PICKLEMANIA

**Look for these other great books
by Jerry Spinelli**

Fourth Grade Rats
Report to the Principal's Office
Do the Funky Pickle
Who Ran My Underwear Up the Flagpole?
The Library Card

PICKLEMANIA

JERRY SPINELLI

SCHOLASTIC INC.

New York Toronto London Auckland Sydney
Mexico City New Delhi Hong Kong Buenos Aires

ISBN 0-590-45447-1

Copyright © 1993 by Jerry Spinelli.
All rights reserved. Published by Scholastic Inc.
SCHOLASTIC, APPLE PAPERBACKS, and associated logos are trademarks and/or registered trademarks of Scholastic Inc.

17 16 15 14 13 12 11 10 9   5 6 7 8 9/0

Printed in the U.S.A.   40

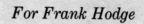
For Frank Hodge

PICKLEMANIA

1

The bus horn was going bonkers, the windchill felt like three hundred below, and forty-eight students were bored or freezing or both.

Oblivious to it all, the man in the white pants and long blue coat and funny three-pointed hat droned on and on: ". . . not enough coats for the whole regiment to drill at once, so while some would wear coats on the parade grounds, others were back at the fires. Even officers had to lead drills in their dressing robes. An infantry regiment consisted of five hundred and eighty-five individuals: four hundred and seventy-seven privates, twenty-seven corporals . . ."

The scene was Valley Forge National Park.

". . . twenty-seven sergeants . . ."

The occasion was a field trip for Miss Billups' two social studies classes.

". . . nine ensigns, eight lieutenants . . ."

The man in the white pants and funny hat was a park ranger, telling them all about the Continental Army's encampment at Valley Forge during the winter of 1777–78.

". . . eight drums, eight fifes . . ."

The honking horn came from the school bus. The driver, known only as Bobo, featured hairy ears and a stomach big enough to hold a full load of wash. He was pounding on the horn because park rules forbade him from keeping the motor on while parked, so he was cold. And because they were supposed to be finished by three o'clock and it was already three-thirty. And because he had to go to the bathroom.

". . . one drum major, one fife major . . ."

"One frozen sixth-grader," muttered Pickles Johnson.

Pickles' friend Eddie Mott giggled. His friend Sunny Wyler grumbled, "I'm so cold I have green icicles hanging from my nose."

Eddie let out a squawk. Classmates turned and giggled. The teacher glared. The ranger droned on: ". . . one quartermaster . . ."

"Quartermaster?" muttered Pickles. "Why didn't they have a whole one?"

This time Eddie shook silently with laughter, thereby momentarily warming himself.

". . . one adjutant, one surgeon, one surgeon's mate . . ."

Ten minutes and fifty horn honks later, the ranger's story came to a halt. He shouldered his musket, looked over his audience, and said, "Any questions?"

Already half the kids had taken a step backward, edging for the bus. No one spoke until Salem Brownmiller raised her hand. "Yes, I have a question." Forty-seven students groaned. Salem looked up from her notebook, in which she had been writing the entire time. "You said one surgeon's mate?"

The ranger nodded. "That's right."

"You mean he was allowed to bring his wife to war?"

The ranger seemed stumped, then he smiled. "In this case 'mate' means assistant, not wife. It's military language."

Salem nodded. "I see." She made more notes. Her notebook was shaded by the wide brim of her floppy, black felt hat. She had seen a picture of her favorite author Willow Wembley wearing such a hat. Since Salem aspired to be a writer — in fact, considered herself already to be one — she was delighted to discover that she herself owned a similar hat; she had worn it only once, on Halloween. She kept it in her book bag and wore it to and from school and all the time at home, indoors and out. With her hat, black writing scarf, and ankle-length skirts, she got plenty of static from other students, but that didn't bother her. In fact, she kind of liked it. The way she figured, artists were supposed to be eccentric and non-conforming, and static from others was a badge that told you that you were doing it right.

When she finished writing, her hand shot up again. The students, by now leaning so severely toward the bus that they were practically horizontal, made mutinous noises. Sunny kicked Salem in the shin. Salem shot her a glance and asked her question. "You said earlier that one of the things they ate was bone soup. Could you give the recipe?"

The ranger blew warmth into his hands. "I'm afraid I don't know it. Maybe you can find it in your library at school."

Salem nodded and jotted; she spoke while writing. "I guess it's safe to say it starts with a bone."

"Yes," agreed the ranger. His lips were blue. His eyes were pleading, *Don't ask another question, please.*

Salem's hand began to rise once more, but it never got above her head. She found her arms pinned, herself wrapped in a bear hug by Sunny, whose voice hissed in her ear, "Say another word and you're dead."

Pickles seized the moment. "Everybody run for the bus!" he shouted, and forty-eight students stampeded for the parking lot.

4

2

Bobo saw them coming. The bus roared to life, the door swung open, the fans delivered cold air along the seats.

Salem Brownmiller and Miss Billups were the last aboard. The moment Miss Billups climbed onto the first step, the door snapped shut, nudging her in the backside and tipping her forward. The students laughed. Miss Billups stepped onto the platform, adjusted her glasses, and scowled at the driver. "I'll thank you to wait until I am *completely* inside before you close the door."

Bobo worked his cigar butt to one side of his mouth, growled, "You're welcome" out the other, and jerked the gearshift into reverse. The bus lurched backward, then forward — fast — with no letup as it careened out of the parking lot and onto Outer Line Drive. By now Miss Billups was sitting in Eddie Mott's lap, and the bus was rocking with laughter.

The teacher stood, spread her feet for balance,

5

grabbed the seat backs on either side, and declared with as much dignity as possible, "Mr. Bobo, you will be reported to the principal." She took a seat.

Bobo said nothing, only worked the cigar butt from side to side. The butt was cold. Out. Dead. Another rule: No smoking on the job. Well, how about a dead butt? That against the rules, too? Let 'em take him to the Supreme Court.

Most of the teachers at Plumstead Middle School hated Bobo. He was obnoxious, cantankerous, and grumpy. He drove recklessly and too fast, yet half the time he was late. He fought with the students and was always complaining. He was a slob. He shaved only once a week. The hair sprouting from his ears was long enough for a Weed Eater. And that brown, chewed on, masticated, smelly stump was forever sticking out of his face.

For the very same reasons, the students loved him. Some even walked across town every morning so they could be picked up along his route.

As the bus flashed past a row of cannon forever pointed toward the British redcoats in Philadelphia, a boy called from the rear, "Hey Bobo, you're going too fast!"

Others joined in:

"Yo Bobo, slow down!"

"Where's the fire?"

"Bobo!"

The students expected two things to happen: (1) The bus would go faster, and (2) Bobo would holler at them, probably tell them about all the mouths he had to feed, and if they were lucky maybe even lay one of his famous curses on them.

"Buh-buh-buh-buh-*Bobo!*"

Sure enough: (1) The bus speeded up, and (2) he hollered at them. "Shut up, back there! I'll slow down when you speed up. Look at this. It's almost four o'clock. I'm gonna be late for work. This ain't my only job, y'know. I got three mouths to feed. Four counting me. I got better things to do than driving you nosepickers around."

This only encouraged the kids to goad him on more.

"Hey Bobo, this air's cold coming outta here!"

"Hey Bo, you're going too slow!"

"Hey yo hobo Bobo!"

Bobo hung a sharp right and the bus squealed into the parking lot of Washington's Headquarters. Ignoring the area reserved for buses, he parked across seven automobile spaces and turned off the motor. He stood and faced the long rows of students. "May a squirrel the size of an elephant sit on your birthday cake," he said and left the bus.

The kids roared for a full minute. Bobo patterned his curses after the old *Tonight Show* with Johnny Carson. They seldom made any sense, but that only made the kids love them more.

7

When they finally stopped laughing, they began to wonder where he went. "Maybe he finally did it," said Eddie Mott. Everyone knew what he meant. Bobo was always threatening to walk off the bus and let the kids drive it, if they thought they were so hot.

"I don't think so," said Pickles. "I think he's going to the bathroom."

While Miss Billups cringed, the students debated: Were they abandoned for good, or just for a bathroom call?

3

A cheer erupted from the bus as Bobo was spotted coming out of the snack and souvenir shop. He climbed aboard and fired up the motor. The parking lot was confusing, with several entrances. He went out the one he thought he had come in, only to realize he was heading back the way they came.

"Hey Bobo," someone shouted, "you're going the wrong way!"

Bobo never admitted to a kid that he was wrong. "I'm taking a shortcut," he called and gunned the gas.

For the next ten minutes the yellow bus barreled about the park, zooming past soldiers' huts and cannon and markers and monuments. At one point the bus found itself atop Mount Misery ("Yo Bobo, what're we doing up here?"), with no place to go but back down.

As they approached the statue of Mad Anthony Wayne, Bobo coughed several times and pulled the bus to a stop. He opened the door and, never leaving the driver's seat, reared back, thrust forward, and sent a spitball out the door.

"Oh, gross!" forty students yelled as one.

Miss Billups looked faint.

Bobo closed the door and drove on. Suddenly Salem Brownmiller was at his side. "You should be ashamed," she told him.

"You should be in your seat," he said. "Go sit down."

"I will when you apologize."

"To who?"

Salem gazed at the rolling hills, bare and brown with grass as dead as the tobacco in Bobo's cigar butt. She pointed. "Them."

Bobo looked. "Huh?"

"The dead," said Salem. "The valiant men who died here so that the United States could be born. This is hallowed ground. This is the birthplace of a nation. They froze and got sick and ate bone soup and died for you, and you spit on them."

"I spit on the street."

"You spit on their memory. You spit on history."

"I'll spit on you if you don't sit down."

Salem tightened her lips; she took a long, loud breath through her nose. "Are you going to apologize?"

Bobo shifted the cigar butt till it pointed at the brown-haired sixth-grader. Then he removed it from his mouth and pronounced the word as though he were blowing a smoke ring: "No."

Salem glared at the bus driver. Her nostrils flared. "Then you may let me out."

"Go sit down," he said.

"You have insulted my country. I will not ride with you."

From her seat Miss Billups reached out to Salem's book bag. "You'd better sit down now, Salem."

Salem turned. "Miss Billups, he's against everything you've been teaching us. He has no respect. This" — she sneered in the driver's direction — "is the reason our country is in trouble."

Before Miss Billups could respond, the bus came to a sudden stop. Car brakes squealed behind. The door flew open. Bobo swept his arm toward the open door and said to Salem, "Have a nice walk. Hold onto your hat."

Shocked at first, Salem quickly recovered. She sniffed, lifted her head high, and walked off the bus.

"Salem!" screeched Miss Billups, but Pickles was already out the door. A half minute later he returned with Salem. With one hand around her wrist, he said to Bobo, "Say you're sorry."

The bus was silent. Miss Billups' eyes and mouth made a trio of ovals on her face. The look on Bobo's face, whatever it was, no one had ever seen before. For a full minute, as traffic backed up and cars honked and swerved past the bus in the middle of the road, Bobo never twitched, never took his eyes from the green-sneakered kid before him. Then, with no apparent movement on his part, the bus door closed with a gasp, and they were rolling again.

4

When the yellow bus finally left the students off at school, Salem, Sunny, Eddie, and Pickles climbed aboard the green one — the pickle-bus, Pickles' green, surfboard-size skateboard-for-four. As they coasted away from the school grounds, Pickles called back to Salem, "I feel a spit coming on. You want to get off and walk?"

"Funny," said Salem. "I can't believe all of you didn't protest with me. That man is a disgrace. He should be fired. If Miss Billups doesn't report him, I think I will."

"He's got three mouths to feed," said Pickles. "You want his kids to starve?"

Salem snorted. "Probably be doing his kids a favor. Then the Board of Health would take them away from him. They'd be better off in an orphanage. How would you like to have that beast as a father?"

"I wouldn't mind," said Sunny. "I think he's funny."

"He probably lets his kids do anything they want," said Eddie.

Pickles said, "You're just jealous, Salem. Because his ears are so hairy he doesn't even need earmuffs in the winter."

Everyone but Salem laughed.

The picklebus wobbled for half a block as the friends laughed and fought for balance.

"Well anyway," said Salem, still wanting to make her point, "it would be one thing if he was in a zoo. He belongs in a cage, not a house. I get the creeps just thinking about being married to him. I don't blame his wife for running away."

"Where is she now?" said Eddie.

"I heard she went to California," said Pickles.

"I heard she's a lady boxer somewhere," said Sunny.

"But really," said Pickles, "if she took off and left him with three mouths to feed, doesn't that make her worse than him?"

Everyone pondered the question as the six wheels hummed over the sidewalk.

Eddie was next to speak. "You know, I was just thinking. I never heard him call them kids. He always just calls them three mouths to feed."

Pickles pulled the bus to a sudden stop. He turned. He nodded. "Hey, you're right. Just mouths to feed. Has anybody ever seen the mouths?"

Three kids stared back at Pickles.

"Maybe they're three monkey mouths," said Sunny.

"Or goldfish," said Eddie.

"Whatever they are," said Salem, "I'll bet they're not human."

The picklebus rolled on.

Sunny said, "I think I'm gonna start wearing a mask when I ride this bus."

"Why?" said Eddie.

"So nobody will recognize me."

"Why do you want to do that?"

"So nobody'll know it's me riding on the same bus with a stupid hat."

Eddie and Pickles cracked up. Salem snipped, "Then maybe I'll wear a mask, too. I feel the same way about your abominable DEATH TO MUSH-ROOMS T-shirt."

"At least everybody wears a shirt," Sunny said.

"Maybe I don't wish to be everybody."

"Maybe you don't wish anybody to see your hair. Maybe it's turning green from mold."

"Maybe she has cooties!" Eddie laughed.

"Maybe someday you'll all be begging for my autograph," said Salem. "Maybe you'll be brag-ging to your children about how you used to be friends with the famous author Salem Jane Brownmiller. And how she used to wear a hat and you used to make fun of her. And how you grew up and amounted to nothing, and you'll wish to your dying day that you had been more like her."

"Goosepoop," said Sunny.

The picklebus rounded a corner. The green-sneakered driver called, "Uh-oh. Trouble ahead."

The three passengers leaned out to look.

5

"Tuh-Tuh-Tuh . . ." Eddie tried to speak but couldn't get far.

"Tuna Casseroli," said Pickles.

"You sure?" said Salem.

"Who else is that wide?" said Sunny.

The body with its back to them a half block ahead was indeed as wide as the sidewalk.

"Looks like he did it," said Pickles.

"He said he would," said Salem.

"What a jerk," said Sunny.

Tuna Casseroli had joined the nickelheads, which meant he had a nickelhead head: hair cut down to a fraction of an inch, with shaved, bald circles all over, a polka-dot effect. Despite the cold, he wore nothing above the waist but a sleeveless T-shirt. Huge red letters spelled the word TUNA across the front and back.

At first it seemed that Tuna was alone. Then he veered to walk along the curb and three other nickelheads appeared; they had been obscured by his bulk.

"Maybe you should turn off," said Eddie.

"Too late," said Pickles.

The first rule of Eddie's life since arriving in middle school was Beware of Nickelheads. The second rule, dating from the time the mammoth eighth-grader dangled him upside down by his ankles, was Beware of Tuna Casseroli. Now that rules one and two had merged, Eddie felt like a fly in Spider Web City.

One of the nickelheads turned. "Hey, Tuna," he called, "look who's coming."

Tuna turned and stopped. He smiled. His cheeks puffed up like two small bellies. "Well, well." He stepped back into the middle of the sidewalk.

The picklebus came to a halt. Four sixth-graders, four grinning nickelheads.

"Howdy," said Tuna. He strolled around the picklebus, took his time doing it. "Nice board you got there. Sure wish I had one."

"Save your pennies," said Pickles.

Tuna stopped strolling and smiling. The other nickelheads circled the bus. Tuna stared at Pickles. He wasn't used to kids staring back at him, but then Pickles Johnson wasn't an ordinary kid. The nickelheads had never been able to scare Pickles, or catch him, or figure him out. And that made them a little unsure of how to deal with him.

But Pickles was not the only passenger who was not afraid of Tuna. "Outta the way, lardbutt," growled Sunny.

This gave Tuna an excuse to forfeit the staring duel to Pickles. He cranked up his grin. "Say please."

Sunny leaned forward and made a pleading face. "Please . . . drop dead."

Tuna laughed. Beneath his shirt, his body shook like a huge, water-filled balloon. He held out his bare arms. "Hey, what's the matter with you wimps?" He reached behind Pickles to where Eddie was trying unsuccessfully to vanish. He felt the thickness of Eddie's winter jacket. "Can't you take a little cold?"

"We don't have all that blubber to protect us," said Sunny.

Tuna smiled like a crocodile. He pointed to Sunny. "If you weren't a girl, I might have to drop you on your head to teach you a lesson."

"If you weren't so ugly," said Sunny, "maybe the zookeeper would stop feeding you."

Pickles laughed first. Then Tuna, then the rest of the nickelheads. While he was laughing, it occurred to Tuna that he had come to the end of the line with this group. He had several choices. He could continue to stand here and let this snot-nosed girl work him over (no); he could hit somebody (tempting, but no); or he could get himself gracefully out of this (okay, but how?).

19

As if in answer to the question, his eyes directed him to the other girl, the one who kept her mouth shut, the one wearing . . . He snatched the black floppy hat from her head, yelled, "Hiyo, nickelheads!" and took off.

For a two-hundred-and-forty-pounder, Tuna Casseroli could move. Before Salem was finished shrieking, "Give me my hat, you bully!" the nickelheads were turning the corner at the end of the block. Also, a fully loaded picklebus was slow to get going.

By the time Pickles had the nickelheads in view, they were racing and hooting past the storefronts of Winter Street. Suddenly, Tuna stopped, looked back, waved the hat grandly in the air, and flipped it over his head. It disappeared onto the roof of a one-story building as the nickelheads went on their way.

Sunny jumped off the bus and ran into the building. In less than a minute, she appeared on the roof. She tossed the hat down to Salem.

When Sunny returned, an obviously relieved Salem said, "I thought you didn't like this hat."

"I don't," said Sunny. "I hate the hat."

"So why did you save it?"

"Because for some stupid reason, you like it. I'm allowed to hate it." She sneered in the direction Tuna had departed. "He's not."

Salem got teary. "Nobody ever had a better best friend." And then she was hugging Sunny.

Sunny put up with it for a few seconds, then said, "Enough already," and disengaged herself. She spoke to all of them. "Did you see what this place is?" She pointed to the large front window. The sign painted across it said KUNG FU ACADEMY. Inside, kids and grown-ups, boys and girls alike in pajamalike white outfits and bare feet, were doing a variety of stylized arm and leg movements.

"I'm going back in," Sunny said and went inside.

6

When Sunny came out, she had a brochure telling all about the Kung Fu Academy. "I'm going to join up," she announced. "I'm taking lessons. I'll be our bodyguard. Nobody'll mess with us then."

No one tried to talk her out of it. Even Salem, who abhorred violence, kept her objections to herself. Everyone recognized that Sunny Wyler and kung fu were a perfect match.

It was dark by the time Pickles dropped off Sunny, then Salem. "Why don't you eat with us," Pickles said to Eddie. "You can call your parents from my house."

That's what they did.

After dinner, they were talking in Pickles' room.

Pickles said, "You going to put a Love Line in *The Wurple?*"

"Nah. You?"

"Not me."

The Wurple was the Plumstead Middle School newspaper. Its name was a blending of the school colors: white and purple. For its Valentine's Day edition, *The Wurple* was devoting a whole page to "Love Lines," one line per customer, for the students to publish their valentine greetings.

"Aren't you going to do one for Sunny?" said Pickles. Eddie had fallen in love with Sunny on the first day of school.

"Nope," said Eddie. "I gave up on her." He went to the window. "Anyway, I don't even deserve her."

"What do you mean? What's bothering you?"

Eddie turned. "What's bothering me? I'll show you what's bothering me." He strode over to Pickles. He rolled up his sleeve and thrust out his arm. "*This* is what's bothering me."

Pickles inspected the arm. "What's the matter with it?"

Eddie pulled it away and rolled his sleeve down. "It's scrawny, that's what's the matter."

"So?"

Eddie screeched, "*See?* You know it. It *is* scrawny!"

"You're the one who said it."

"You agreed!"

Pickles sighed. He sat down beside Eddie. "What's the problem?"

"The problem," Eddie whined, "is I'm too little. I try and I try to be a regular sixth-grader, 'cause

23

I'm not in grade school anymore. I tell myself over and over" — he punched the mattress — "you're in middle school now, you're in middle school now, but . . . but . . . I still look like I'm in first grade!" His voice was quivering, his eyes watery.

Pickles laid a hand on Eddie's knee. He chuckled. "Take my word for it, you don't look like first grade."

"Well," Eddie sniffed, "fourth grade." He thrust his face into Pickles'. "And that's no kidding. I know fourth-graders who are bigger than me."

Pickles flapped his hand. "Ah, that's no big deal. I'll bet most of them are girls. A lot of girls are taller than boys at our age."

"It's not just taller." Eddie yanked up his sleeve again, then the other sleeve. Then he pulled his pants up over his knees. He pulled his shirttail to his shoulders. "It's scrawny. I'm the scrawniest, skinniest, shrimpiest, runtiest kid in all of Plumstead Middle School." He jutted his jaw. "And you know it."

The sight before him — his best friend looking like something from a 1920s' bathing beach — sent Pickles into gales of laughter. Each time he tried to stop, he took another look and had to laugh some more. And the dead serious look on Eddie's face didn't help any. Finally, fearing a hernia, Pickles reached out and pulled down Eddie's shirt, pant legs, and sleeves. He then flopped onto his back to recuperate, like a distance runner after a race.

Eddie sat on the bed. "I gotta bulk up."

"Why don't you just wait," said Pickles. "You're only eleven. You have seven more years to grow."

"Seven more years for Tuna Casseroli to hang me upside down. Seven more years of torture from the nickelheads. I'll be dead!"

"Well," said Pickles, "you still can't do it overnight. You could eat ten times a day for a year and not get as big as Tuna's left leg."

Eddie held out pleading hands. "All I want right now is to weigh ninety pounds. That's my dream in life."

Pickles sat up, studied his pal. "Stand up." Eddie stood. "You don't weigh ninety?"

"Not even close."

"You're not the shortest kid in school."

"I *told* you, I'm not talking short, I'm talking scrawny. Bony." He held out his wrist. "Put your hand around there." Pickles curled his fingers around Eddie's wrist. They could have almost gone around twice.

Eddie pulled his wrist away. "See? I take after my mother. I have the world's littlest bones. The only difference between me and a skeleton is skin."

Pickles was in thought. "You say you'd like to weigh ninety?"

"Right now I'd be happy with eighty."

"How about a hundred?"

"Huh?"

"Would you feel good if you looked down at a scale and it said one hundred pounds?"

"It ain't gonna — "

"Just *would* you?"

Eddie shrugged. "Yeah. Sure."

Pickles popped up and dragged Eddie to his closet. He began pulling out clothes and putting them on Eddie. A sweatshirt. A sweater. A winter jacket. Another jacket. Two pair of pants. Boots (after pulling off Eddie's sneakers). And hats, five of them stacked atop one another.

Pickles looked around. "You bring a book bag?"

"No."

Pickles got his, dumped more books into it, and hung it over Eddie's shoulder. He then led Eddie into the bathroom. With the green toe of his sneaker, he pushed the scale out from under the sink. "Okay, climb on."

Eddie got on. The pointer moved past 70 . . . past 80 . . . 90 . . . and stopped at 92.

Pickles ordered, "Don't move," and rushed off. In seconds he was back with a typewriter, an old black Underwood. "My mother's," he said. "Hold out your arms." He placed the typewriter in Eddie's arms. Eddie's knees buckled, but he held on. Pickles crouched like a spotter in a weight room. The pointer shot past 100. Eddie pushed out the typewriter so he could see.

"One hundred and four pounds," Pickles announced. "How's it feel?"

Eddie gave Pickles a disgusted look. He handed back the typewriter and stepped off the scale. "It feels stupid. How dumb do you think I am?"

"Just thought I'd try a little psychology. Guess it didn't work."

Pickles left with the typewriter. When he returned, he said, "We'll start bulking you up tomorrow. In the meantime" — there was a sly grin on his lips, a gleam in his eyes — "are you ready to see something in the basement?"

Eddie was puzzled at first, then his eyes widened. "It's done?"

"Almost."

"You're gonna let me see it?"

"You'll be the first."

Thoughts of pounds vanished as Eddie clapped, "All *right*!" and the two of them raced downstairs.

7

Eddie spun in the middle of the basement. "Where?"

Pickles pointed to a corner in the back. "There." A long, low something was hidden under an olive green tarpaulin.

Eddie approached with the reverence of a kid discovering his first whisker. He stood before the tarp.

"Take it off," said Pickles.

Eddie gave a tug, and the tarp slid to the floor. Eddie gasped. He could not speak.

Pickles came up behind him. "What do you think?"

Eddie wagged his head. "Wow."

"All I have to do is paint on the name."

"What's that?"

"Pickleboggan."

It was unlike anything the world had seen. Part sled, part boat, part bus, part pure Pickles. No fewer than six sleds, modified and wired together, formed the deck. From the deck rose plywood walls two feet high. In the stern was a coxswain's perch and a homemade pennant showing a pickle schussing downhill on skis; in the bow, a tiller for steering and a motorcycle headlight. The runners were painted silver; the rest, of course, was green.

Eddie said, "Did Sunny and Salem see it yet?"

"You're the first."

"The first kid?"

"The first human."

Eddie wanted to weep at the honor of it. "Wait till they see."

"Yeah," said Pickles. "But it's not for seeing, it's for sledding."

Eddie smiled wistfully. "I was just picturing us going down Heller's. The four of us."

"A green flash."

"I'll bet this baby could do fifty."

"Sixty if the snow's got some ice on it."

They stared at the great, green snow cruiser, each conjuring up a picture of Heller's Hill, the best sledding hill in town, maybe in the world. It had the two chief requirements of a Class A hill: It was both steep and long. A mile long, some said. They saw themselves ripping down the roller coaster slope, vaporizing snow, firing ice to diamonds, screaming, screaming, then, at Mach 1, a sudden silence, outracing their own voices, sledding into history. . . .

"You dream of weighing ninety," said Pickles. "I dream of snow."

Eddie nodded sadly. "Is it possible to have a winter without snow?"

There was no answer. And there was no snow on Heller's Hill. This had been the great tragedy of the winter. Here they were, in the beginning of February, and not so much as a single flake had fallen to earth. No snow days off. No snowballs. No sledding.

The tarp crackled like bottled thunder as Pickles shook it out and drew it over the sled. "I'm making a solemn vow right now — until it snows, nobody else will lay eyes on this thing. I swear."

8

Next day was Saturday. In February it had another name: Mallday.

The four friends, flush with allowances and advances, were dumped off by Sunny's mother at the entrance to Kingswood Mall. Before they went inside, Pickles looked up at the sky. He shielded his eyes from the sun. "Not a cloud in sight." He held his jacket open. "Not even cold."

Eddie pointed to the time and temperature display above the entrance. "Look."

The temperature was 56 degrees Fahrenheit.

Eddie grumped, "It's never going to snow."

Sunny said, "Maybe winter's over. That was it."

They went inside.

Salem asked Pickles, "Is your super-duper secret sled ready yet?"

"Almost. Just have to paint the name on."

"What's that?"

"You'll see."

"Will it hold all four of us?"

"Four of us?" blurted Eddie. "It'll hold half the school!"

The two girls stopped walking and stared at Pickles, who glared at Eddie, who winced and went, "Oops."

"He saw it," said Sunny.

"You said nobody could see it till it was finished," said Salem.

"I just gave him a peek," said Pickles. "It was a special case."

"So we're not special?"

Pickles rolled his eyes. "He was feeling bad bad about something, so I just did it to cheer him up."

"I feel bad about something, too," said Sunny. "How about cheering me up?"

Pickles shook his head. "No more peeks. Until it snows. I took a vow. I'm not even going to look at it myself."

Sunny stepped up to Pickles; she poked him in the chest. "Well, I've got news for you, buster. Whenever it does snow, don't come around for me. You couldn't *beg* me to look at that thing. You couldn't force me if you drove up in a tank. I'll sew my eyes shut first. I'll nail a football helmet to my face backwards." She started to pull Salem away. "Come on."

Salem resisted. "Wait a minute. Eddie, why were you feeling bad?"

Salem loved to hear about other people's problems and feelings. As a practicing author, she viewed all of humankind as a great research library from which she would gather material for the novels in her future. She thus felt entitled to know everyone's business, kind of like a psychiatrist or doctor.

Eddie, on his part, found it almost impossible to keep his business to himself. He was a terrible liar and a hopeless denier. His timid resistance was no match for such a stern and relentless interrogator as Salem Brownmiller.

Pickles knew this, of course, and attempted to drag Eddie off.

"Eddie, tell me," said Salem, herself tugged in the opposite direction by Sunny.

Even as he was being dragged away, Eddie's head tilted toward Salem as though she had him lassoed.

"Eddie," she repeated, locking onto his eyes, freezing them.

Eddie spoke as if to a hypnotist. "I'm too scrawny. I gotta bulk up."

Sunny cackled in full voice: "He wants to be a *hunk!*"

All around them mall walkers turned and stared and tittered.

Pickles growled at Eddie, "You satisfied, flushmouth?" and dragged him away.

9

As they walked off in the opposite direction from the guys, Salem said to Sunny, "So, what are *you* feeling bad about?"

Sunny bristled. "Hey, don't try that stuff here. Maybe it works on the hunk, but not me."

"Who's trying stuff? I'm asking a question, that's all."

"Why?"

"Because I'm interested."

"Interested in writing a book."

"I'm interested in you."

"Sure."

Salem stopped and stomped her foot. "I *am*. You saved my hat." She pulled off her hat and wagged it in Sunny's face. "I *care*."

Sunny resumed walking. Her jaw kept its hard set, but her eyes softened. "I'm not allowed to join the Kung Fu Academy."

"Oh," said Salem, "I'm sorry."

Sunny sneered, "No, you're not." Salem just

stared. "You don't want me to join either, and you know it."

"I didn't say that."

"You're just like my mother. You think everything's violence. You think stabbing a lima bean with a fork is violence. You don't think people should learn to defend themselves. You think if somebody comes up and smacks me, I'm supposed to say" — she fluttered her fingertips and made her voice mincy — " 'Oh thank you, that was nice. Here's my other cheek, do it again. Make it a good one this time.' "

Salem clenched her teeth to keep a straight face. "It's not a laughing matter."

"Who says it is? Do I look like I'm laughing? All I'm saying is" — she poked Salem in the chest — "I don't care what she says. I'm doing it."

"You can't."

"Watch me."

Sunny marched off.

"Where are you going?"

"What do you care?"

Salem groaned and watched her incorrigible friend disappear into Sears. She was about to follow when her eye was caught by a display in Thrift Drug. The entire window to the right of the door was filled with hearts: heart-shaped boxes of valentine candy. They ranged from simple little $3.95 cardboard boxes with four chocolates to a huge lace-and-satin-covered wonder with a fat lavender bow and a $39.95 price tag.

Was there a heart-shaped candy box in her future? Salem wondered. At the moment, she would have been quite happy — thrilled, in fact — with the $3.95 version. Heck, she'd settle for a love line in *The Wurple*'s soon-to-be published Valentine's Day edition. Was some secret admirer even now, pencil in hand, composing his love line to her? Miss O'Malley was *The Wurple*'s faculty adviser. In her classroom sat the red-papered box with a slit in top for depositing love lines. The box had already been filled and emptied once. There was a lot of love out there.

Salem pulled herself away and entered Sears. She found Sunny in, of all places, men's wear, looking through the pajamas.

"Present for your father?" said Salem.

"No."

"Who?"

"Me."

Sunny looked at every pair on the counter. "No white."

"Pajamas don't usually come in white," said Salem. "Especially men's. And why are you looking for men's pajamas anyway?"

Sunny didn't answer. She went back through the small sizes, intensely inspecting each plastic-wrapped package. She pulled out a pair of plain, collarless pajamas the color of tea with milk in it.

The tag said BEIGE. She held it up to Salem. "What do you think?"

"*Think?*" Salem squeaked. "How am I supposed to know *what* to think? I don't even know what you're *doing!*"

"My, my," said Sunny. She touched Salem's nose with her fingertip and jerked it away as if the nose were hot. "Touchy, aren't we?" She walked off.

She led Salem through men's clothing, through women's clothing, and was heading into the dressing room when Salem stopped her. "Where are you going?"

"Where's it look like?"

"You don't try on pajamas in the store."

"That so?"

"And you especially don't try on men's pajamas in the women's dressing room."

"Really?"

Sunny marched down to the last stall on the right, stepped in, and closed the curtain. Salem remained firmly at the entrance. She would not involve herself in this nonsense any further.

After a minute or so, Sunny's voice drifted out: "Salem, come here."

Salem folded her arms. "No."

"*Salem!*"

Salem went. When she opened the curtain, she found Sunny wearing the pajamas; her socks, sneakers, and jeans were piled on the floor. Sunny assumed what she believed to be a martial-arts stance: torso turned over widely spread legs, elbows high and crooked, hands flat, scissorlike. "What do you think?"

"I think they're too big."

"They're supposed to be big. Roomy. So you're free to move — like lightning." Sunny flashed her scissory hands.

"If you're not allowed to join the academy," Salem said, "what's the point?"

"The point is, I'll be my own academy. I'll teach myself." Over Salem's objections, she untied Salem's black writing scarf and tied it around her waist. "See? I'm a black belt already." She assumed a chopping stance over an imaginary board; she reared back; she drove the edge of her hand down mightily: "Hai-YAH!" The imaginary board fell to the floor in two imaginary pieces.

That's when they heard the giggle.

10

They looked at the curtain. Nothing. Then they looked under the curtain, in the twelve inches of space between its bottom edge and the floor. The sideways face of a little boy grinned up at them. Also showing beneath the curtain was a hand, clutching a braided, half-eaten licorice stick; his grinning teeth were black from it.

All of this registered in the girls' minds in a second or two. In less time than that, like a lizard, the black-toothed grinner darted under the curtain on his belly, snatched Sunny's jeans with his own "Hai-YAH!," and took off.

Sunny lit out after him. "You're in pajamas!" Salem called, as if anyone ever listened to her. By the time she emerged from the dressing room, the boy was racing through lingerie and underwear, display trees of bikinis wobbling and wiggling in his wake. Alarmed shoppers were swinging their heads to his shouts of "Hai-YAH! . . . Hai-YAH!" Those who continued to stare saw a black-haired girl in hot pursuit and men's pajamas, yelling, "You're dead! . . . You're horsemeat!"

Salem wanted to race after them, but her dignity forbade it. She set off at a fast walk, following their shrieking voices and the shoppers' turning heads. She made a point of looking at the merchandise as she passed, lest anyone think she was associated with the two stampeding delinquents. When she heard the volume of their voices abruptly bloom, she knew they had burst from Sears into the open mall.

Sunny chased the thief past Fluf 'N Stuf, Woolworth, Foot Locker, store after store, hips slamming from side to side to avoid the oncoming shoppers. The kid was small as a squirrel and just as shifty, quick as a fly. She thought she had him at Hickory Farms, where the little fleabrain slowed down to snatch a free sample of bratwurst (how appropriate!); but when she reached out for him, all she came away with was a fistful of sticky black licorice.

On through the food court — Mexican Delite, Pita Pockets, La Roma Pizza — sodas spilling, trays clattering, the kid yelling, "Hai-YAH!," the voice of the mall intercom intoning over the tumult: "Code Ten food court . . . Code Ten food court."

Out of the food court, around the soft pretzel kiosk, up the down escalator, down the up escalator, Shirts Plus, Shazzam Comics, Gold Medal

Sporting Goods, on toward the other end of the mall, where the pool in front of Penney's geysered skyward in the middle like a water fountain for a giant. The kid never hesitated, never flinched for an instant, but dashed straight into the pool. (Something far below Sunny's thoughts took notice and registered a kindred approval.)

As Sunny slowly circled the pool, like a stalking lion, the kid kept the geyser between himself and her. He held her jeans above his head and so far had not allowed them to get wet. His antic mischief had given way to a casual smugness, the confidence that comes to a little kid who has gone where anyone older or bigger dare not follow. He did not know Sunny Wyler.

Seeing that the kid was not about to come out on his own, Sunny waded in after him. The kid seemed both terrified and delighted at once. He screamed. He reared back and flung her jeans high; they landed upon the roiling peak of the geyser and, for a good five seconds, as the gathering audience whistled and clapped, the pants did a funky, disembodied dance before joining the rain in its fall to the pool.

Sunny and the kid circled the geyser, and suddenly there were two new boys splashing into the pool, yelling and laughing and smacking small floods of water at her and the first kid and each other. The crowd was going wild, pennies were copperraining into the water, the mall intercom

42

was repeating: "Code Ten Penney's fountain . . . Code Ten Penney's fountain." And outlouding everything was a booming voice, a familiar voice: "Get outta there, you nosepickers! You got five seconds!"

Salem arrived in time to join Pickles and Eddie in the applauding, pennypitching crowd. "You hear that?" she said. The three of them turned to see first a stomach, then a man with hairy ears emerge from the crowd and step to the edge of the pool. He spiked a stiff finger to the floor. "Now!"

Eddie gasped, "Bobo!"

"The three mouths to feed," said Salem.

Pickles chuckled in wonder. "They *are* monkeys."

11

It had been a day of adventure for Salem, a day to nourish a young writer. New vistas of human behavior had been revealed to her. It amazed her that Sunny could be her best friend and yet repeatedly surprise her.

The security people had shown up while the three monkeys, ignoring their father's blustering orders, filled their pockets with pool pennies. They, along with Sunny, were herded off to security headquarters by four semi-police-looking guys.

Bobo kept ranting at his kids, saying he was going to let them rot in jail. Salem, Pickles, and Eddie followed in their wet tracks. For a joke, Pickles suggested to one of the guards that he'd better handcuff Sunny. Eddie just gawked in wonder. This was the closest he had ever been to crime.

Bobo was allowed to follow into the security office. Friends of the perpetrators had to wait outside. The door was shut. Noting that the Book Bin was across the way, Salem went over to browse, and who did she meet but Miss Billups.

"Well, well," said the teacher, "I was just thinking of you. I just picked this up." It was a paperback titled *Valley Forge: A Soldier's Diary*. She held it out. "Would you like it?"

Salem gasped, "For me?"

"It's too seldom I get a student as interested in history as you are." She clawed Salem's shoulder playfully. "I want to keep you in my clutches. Besides" — she lowered her voice to a whisper — "I got it off the dollar ninety-five table."

Salem was overcome. She hugged her teacher.

Miss Billups was carrying a handled shopping bag. Salem could not help noticing one of the items inside: a heart-shaped candy box. "Sending that to your secret valentine?" she said kiddingly.

Miss Billups did not react at first, then she laughed. "Yes, my little nephew. He's my cutie."

"To tell you the truth," said Salem, "I think I'd even settle for a valentine from a relative." Then she remembered the dinky little scrap she received in second grade from her cousin Harold. It showed a cowboy lassoing a horsy-looking heart. She found out later that Aunt Helen had made Harold do it. "Wait a minute," she said, "I take that back." She and Miss Billups shared a big laugh.

Then Sunny and the guys had shown up. The

mall people had lent Sunny a gray sweatsuit, which she had to return. The four of them went back to Sears to fetch Sunny's shoes and socks, Salem took back her writing scarf, Sunny's mother came to get them, and at last it was over.

And now, well into Saturday night, a new adventure occupied Salem. As she lay on her bed reading *A Soldier's Diary*, she was transported back to the terrible winter of 1777–78 and the life of a nineteen-year-old private named Patrick Wister. She shivered with him in the merciless cold. She hungered with him as he boiled bone and scraps for soup. She suffered with him through the fever and celebrated with him when General Washington rationed a few ounces of grog to the troops for Christmas.

But most of all she shared Patrick's longing as he wrote loving letters to his fiancé Abigail Norton in Portsmouth, Virginia. She feared his fears and wondered his wonderings. From the *Diary*'s first page to the last, Patrick received not one letter in return from Abigail. Why? Had his letters not reached her? Was she angry? Ill? Wounded? Worse? Did she still love him? "A hundred times a day," he wrote, "I cry out in silence to the gray sky above, Do you yet wait for me?"

And each time she read it, Salem cried out (not so silently), "Yes, Patrick, I am here! I will wait for you forever!" She read, wept, cried out, read, wept, cried out. She composed a letter, with her father's fountain pen, pledging her love and reassuring him and begging him to return home safely to her.

She felt the cruel emptiness of uncompleted history, as the afterword informed her that the diary was the sole trace on earth left by Patrick Wister; nothing was known of either him or Abigail Norton from that winter onward.

Well after midnight Salem lay down to sleep on the floor. Thinking of Patrick on his hard planked bunk, how could she do any less?

As often happened when the lights went out, Salem's imagination came on. She imagined a ghost story. It was the day *The Wurple*'s Valentine's Day edition came out. As Salem read the "Love Lines" page, she saw something that at first stopped her heart, then sent it wildly pounding:

"SB. I'll love you forever. PW."

12

The picklebus was in the basement for repairs Monday morning, so the picklekids caught the school bus at Eddie's corner. It had been over a month since they had taken the yellow one, and they were surprised to discover a new driver.

"Bobo!" declared Pickles as he climbed aboard. "This isn't your route, is it?"

"No," growled Bobo through his mutilated cigar butt, "it's my grandmother's."

"Eddie and I have to raise the flag, you know. We can't be late."

"I'll write ya a note," snarled Bobo. "Sit down." The kids sat down.

"So," said Salem perkily, "who wants to camp out with me?"

She got stares but no takers.

"What's this?" said Pickles. "You're not exactly the camp-out type."

"Yeah," snickered Sunny, "if you'll remember."

On a weekend in October, Sunny's family had

taken Salem along to a campground. Salem was so jumpy at night that she wouldn't calm down until she was allowed to squeeze into Sunny's sleeping bag. Even then, she kept flinching at every little noise and imagined that assorted nocturnal rodents were keeping company in the bag with them. "Never again," a sleepless Sunny had vowed when they got home.

Salem flicked her hand. "Oh, that was different. I wasn't motivated. This is history. We'll do it just like Valley Forge."

"You going to build a hut?" said Eddie. He popped several peanuts into his mouth.

"Well, no, not exactly. But we can have a tent. Sunny has tents. And we'll make a fire and bone soup and write diaries and do all the things they did."

"Like freeze," said Pickles.

"Not if it stays like this. We're having a heat wave."

Pickles moaned, "You got that right."

"My mother said the temperature's going over sixty today," Eddie reported, popping more peanuts.

Pickles shook his head forlornly. "George Washington got the winter we wanted."

They looked out the bus windows. All four longed for snow. Only three wanted it for sledding.

"We won't do it till it turns cold again," said

49

Salem. "We want it as much like the winter of 1778 as possible. We have to suffer at least a little."

Sunny scowled. "You suffer in the tent, I'll suffer in my bed at home."

Eddie yelped, "Hey!" and pointed out the window. "It's Raymond Hall!"

The four of them scooted to the back window. Raymond Hall, a sixth-grade classmate, was racing after the bus, cheeks puffing, book bag flying. He was falling farther behind with every step.

Pickles called up the aisle, "Bobo, you didn't stop for Raymond Hall."

"Wasn't nobody there," growled Bobo. "You ain't there, the bus don't stop. This ain't a taxi."

Fortunately, the next corner was a route stop, with five kids waiting. By the time the last one got on, Raymond Hall had caught up. He staggered aboard and collapsed on the front seat.

Sunny held out her hand to Eddie. "Gimme some peanuts."

Eddie gave her one.

Sunny's eyes widened. "Wow, can you spare it?"

"It's bulk-up food," said Pickles. "We designed a diet for him."

"Peanuts for a peanut, huh?"

A laugh escaped from Salem before she caught herself.

"Well," drawled Sunny, "I got news for ya. He's never gonna be big enough to do this." She placed the peanut on the seat back in front of her. She stood. She flattened her hand. Three times she swung the edge of her hand down to within a hair's width of the peanut, each time drawing in a long, whistling breath. Then, suddenly, a mighty chop and a "Hai-YAH!" The peanut was dust.

The bus stopped. Several sixth-graders got on, then a big kid. A *real* big kid. Only it wasn't a kid.

"Miss Billups!" cried Salem.

The teacher came down the aisle and took a seat in front of them. "What are you doing here?" said Salem.

"Did your car break?" said Eddie.

"Break *down*, halfahunk," said Sunny.

The teacher turned in her seat to face them. "No, my car's fine." She glanced toward the front of the bus; she spoke in a whisper. "I'm doing undercover work. The principal has asked me to ride the bus for a week to monitor the bus driver and report back to him. That man is a menace to the school and the community, and he would have been fired a long time ago, except we don't have enough bus drivers as it is. And then he's got those three little mouths to feed."

"Hah!" exclaimed Sunny. "Somebody ought to feed *them* to the boa constrictor in the pet store."

Suddenly horns were blaring all around, brakes were screeching. The kids looked out. Pickles called: "Hey, Bobo, this is a one-way street!"

Someone screamed: "We're all gonna die!"

Half the bus screamed. Bobo yelled, "Shaddap, nosepickers, or I'll dump ya all off here!" The bus careened through a right turn, jumped a curb, sent thirty-nine students and one teacher bouncing off their seats, and went roaring down the narrowest street the passengers had ever seen.

Pickles called: "Yo, Bobo, this is an *alley*!"

"Shortcut," answered Bobo.

Garages and backyards went by. The right bumper caught a carelessly placed metal trash can and sent it flying with a racket like New Year's Eve.

Miss Billups had taken out a spiral notebook and was writing it all down. She kept muttering, "A menace . . . a menace . . ."

Another jumped curb and the bus was back on a street.

"Yo, Bobo," called Pickles, "this isn't our route. You're going the wrong way. You're missing people."

No reply came from the driver's seat. The bus went up one street, down another. It zoomed past students frantically waving on corners. At one point it looped through another township. Other school buses passed. They were empty.

"We're late!" someone screamed.

Sixth-graders began to groan and cry; eighth-graders pounded the walls and shouted, "All *riiiight!*"

By the time the bus pulled into the school driveway, Mr. Brimlow, the principal, was waiting. He placed himself at the bus door as it opened and announced, "Sir" — a busful of ears perked up at the absurdity of calling Bobo sir — "you shall report to Late Room at two thirty-five. The rest of you are excused to first class."

The bus emptied in seconds to a chorus of cheers. Left outside were one principal sternly staring, one teacher closing a notebook, and one bus driver chewing slyly on a cigar stump and closing the door.

13

E ddie burped.
    Twice in math. Four times in social studies. A record seven times in music. In English, only once, but that one outdid the other thirteen combined.

It happened while he was standing and reciting lines from "The Raven" by Edgar Allan Poe, as directed by Miss O'Malley. When he came to the line, "Quoth the Raven, 'Nevermore,' " it came out:

"Quoth the Raven, *Brrraaaaawwgh!*"

It took Miss O'Malley ten minutes to settle down the class. It took her two seconds to say, "Detention Room after school, Edward Mott."

Salem heard none of this. *The Wurple* had just been distributed, and she could not help losing herself in the "Love Lines" section while sitting in class. So many students had submitted valentines that "Love Lines" had been expanded to two full pages.

There were dozens and dozens of messages from sixth-, seventh-, and eighth-graders. Some carried full names, some initials, some code names:

"Steph, I love you. Ron."

"RT, I am yours. JY."

"Bumble, Bee my honey. Daisy."

As the bell rang to end the period, a particular item caught Salem's eye. It was toward the bottom of the second page. It read:

SB. Be my valentine? AK.

The kids all thought Eddie was burping on purpose. He wasn't. Since he had begun his new bulk-up diet, his whole system had gone flooey. After the peanuts, he had nibbled his way through bags of bagel bits, banana chips, and raisins. The plan, designed by Pickles, was to eat constantly, every waking minute. The burps were his body's protest.

Though Eddie had always admired the great burpmasters of his generation, he had never been much of a burper himself. It was hard for him to tell when one was coming on. It usually took him by surprise and was out of his mouth long before he could stifle it.

Pickles greeted him on the way to lunch. "Hey, it's the burpster. Burpman. Burpalator."

"I never counted on this," said Eddie. "Is there something that can make me stop?"

"I'll work on it."

"I never had a detention in my life."

"Just the price you're paying for bulking up. It'll be worth it."

"What if my parents find out? Will it go on my report card, the detention?"

Pickles winked at Sunny and Salem, who had joined them. "It'll go on your report card — and your school record."

"And a copy of it goes to the police department," added Sunny. "It follows you the rest of your life."

Pickles' and Sunny's straight faces collapsed at the sight of Eddie's wide, gullible eyes. "Just kidding." Pickles laughed and clamped Eddie in a headlock that served, among sixth-grade boys, as a hug.

"Where's Salem?" said Sunny.

Pickles looked around. "Don't know. Let's eat. She'll find us."

Salem, as it happened, was in the Music Room instrument closet, trying to catch her breath. Her heart was thumping like a bass drum.

This was no midnight phantom fantasy. *The Wurple* clutched in her fist was real. The print on the page, the words — all thrillingly real. "SB . . . SB . . . SB . . ." she kept whispering to the clarinet cases. SB. Salem Brownmiller.

Who else could it be? She knew of at least one other SB in school, a Sarah Berkheimer, also in sixth grade. Was SB Sarah Berkheimer? Salem pictured Sarah in her mind's eye. Did Sarah look like someone to whom something this momentously romantic would happen? In a word — no.

How many other SB's were there? Salem thought of going to the office and asking to see the enrollment roster. Narrow it down to the B's, eliminate the boy B's, eliminate all but the girl SB's, eliminate Sarah Berkheimer. Would that leave anyone but herself?

It began to dawn on Salem that it didn't matter. There could be twenty other SB's, but all her instincts told her that this was no matter for enrollment rosters. This was destiny. This was romance. She had been chosen. She was Cupid's bull's-eye. She felt it. She knew it. SB had to be — could only be — herself.

Now . . . *who was AK?*

At the lunch line, Eddie held back. "I don't know," he said. "I'm not very hungry."

"That's why you're so tiny," said Sunny. "You eat like a bird."

Eddie snapped, "I've been eating all day, that's why I'm not hungry. And I'm not tiny."

"You're teeny."

"I'm not!"

"You're weeny."

Pickles sealed Sunny's mouth with the palm of his hand. "She's raggin' you. Just keep thinking of the day when you'll be big enough to beat her up."

Sunny laughed, but with her mouth sealed shut, the laugh burst from her nose, leaving nostril juice on Pickles' hand. Pickles jerked his hand away, screeched, "Eeeeww!" and wiped it on Sunny's DEATH TO MUSHROOMS T-shirt. Sunny slugged Pickles in the arm. Eddie laughed.

In the lunch line Pickles picked out milk and a dessert for Eddie, who had brought the rest from home. At the table, while the others tore into their tacos, Eddie pulled two sandwiches from his book bag.

Sunny exclaimed, "Chocolate bread?"

"Pumpernickel," said Pickles. "It's better for you."

The others had finished their first tacos, and Eddie still hadn't taken a bite. "Well," said Sunny, "aren't you going to eat?"

Pickles reached over and unwrapped the sandwiches. He handed half of one to Eddie. Eddie held it as though it were a live hand grenade. Sunny grabbed the other half and opened it. She screamed and slammed it shut. "What is it?"

Pickles said matter-of-factly, "Peanut butter and mayonnaise. A protein bomb." He lifted Eddie's hand to his mouth. "Eat."

Sunny steered her eyes elsewhere. "I'm afraid to ask. What's in the other one?"

"Parsley," said Pickles.

"Parsley? That's all? A parsley sandwich?"

"Iron," said Pickles. "There's more iron in a sprig of parsley than in a porterhouse steak." He opened the sandwich for display. "That's worth about what . . . ten steaks there."

Sunny snorted, "Ironman Mott."

Eddie forced down the last bite just as lunch ended. On the way out, Pickles said, "Feel yourself getting any bigger?"

Eddie burped. "Yeah, my stomach."

Pickles slapped Eddie on the back, prompting another burp.

Sunny said, "Where the heck is Salem?"

At that moment Salem was walking out of the main office. Posing as a reporter for *The Wurple*, she had persuaded the secretary, Mrs. Wilburham, to let her see a list of students whose last names began with K.

There were eight K's in Plumstead. Five of them were boys; of those, two were AK's: Avery Kribble and Alan Kent. Avery Kribble was an obnoxious lunkhead sixth-grader. He never took a bath. The only thing dirtier than his body was his mouth. He was always in trouble, and the only people who liked him were nickelheads. He was totally incapable of writing — or feeling — a Love Line.

In a daze, too stunned to feel anything, Salem left the office with one name on her lips. "Alan Kent." She sipped it, as she would a new, exotic tropical juice. "Alan Kent." She nibbled it, as she would an unidentified piece of candy from a heart-shaped box of chocolates. "Alan Kent." She had never heard the name, and suddenly it was as though she had never heard any other. She knew nothing of him. Except one thing.

Whoever Alan Kent was, he loved her.

For Eddie, last period of the day was Study Hall. With ten minutes left in the period, he asked to go to the bathroom and was excused. He prayed that the teacher would not ask why he was taking his book bag along. She didn't.

He hadn't really wanted to use the bathroom, but it was the only place that offered both water and privacy. Well, water for sure; privacy maybe, if no big kids came in to terrorize him, which was why he hadn't been crazy about using the bath-room in the first place.

He set his book bag on the sink and pulled out the can of Moocho Malt. He and Pickles had bought it at the mall on Saturday. Moocho Malt was a powdered concoction that you mixed with water to make a shake "Packed," the can said, "With the Stuff to Make You MASSIVE!" Eddie got the shivers just thinking of that word — MAS-SIVE — applied to himself. He had always been identified with words like "little" and "skinny" and "small." "Massive," on the other hand, brought to mind Arnold Schwarzenegger, King Kong, mountains, and the planet Jupiter. Eddie Mott . . . massive? It seemed all wrong, misplaced, scary.

But thrilling, too. Massive Eddie Mott. In the boys' room mirror he imagined himself growing, swelling hugely, Moocho Malted mass bursting against cord and vein, his bare chest invading the next mirror, his nipples the size of pancakes . . .

He opened the can. He took the plastic glass from his bag. A hand clamped around his wrist. A voice said, "Waddaya got there, runt?"

14

Eddie did not bother to turn. In the mirror he saw two grinning nickelheads. One was Baloney, the other was Salami. Nickelheads had weird names. They insisted the names were on their birth certificates, but Eddie doubted that. Eighth-graders found nickelhead names funny; sixth-graders found them frightening.

The hand released Eddie's wrist and picked up the can. "Hey, Salami, look at this."

"What is it?"

Baloney studied the can. "Moocho Malt."

Salami was swinging from a stall door. "Moooo-cho? What's that? Cow food?" He cackled at his own joke.

Baloney studied the can some more. "Says it makes you mass . . . mass . . . ive. What's that mean?"

"It means big, peanut brain. Like bodybuilders."

Baloney's grin got wider and crookeder. He

crowed to the world, "He wants to be big! He wants muscles!" He read the can some more. "Like a chocolate shake . . . just add water."

Baloney grabbed the plastic glass out of Eddie's hand. He opened the can, pulled the dispenser from the chocolaty powder, dumped three heaping scoopfuls into the glass, added water, stirred with one of Eddie's pencils, and said, "Okay, muscles, drink up."

Eddie drank up. What the heck, he was going to anyway.

Then Baloney made him another shake.

"Only supposed to drink one," said Eddie.

Baloney scowled: "Drink."

"I can't. I'm full. I'm stuffed." He burped.

Baloney pressed the glass against Eddie's nose: "Drink."

Eddie took a deep breath, closed his eyes, drank.

Baloney made him another: "Drink."

Eddie burped. He flatly protested: "No."

Suddenly Salami was with Baloney — a cold cut sandwich — both of them inches from his face. They pronounced together: "Drink."

Eddie imagined himself to be a balloon one puff from bursting. But he had no choice. Trembling under the nickelheads' cold gaze, swallow by swallow he drained the glass. He could see the headlines:

STUDENT FOUND DEAD FROM
OVERDOSE OF MOOCHO MALT

At that moment things began to happen very quickly.

The bell rang. Baloney said, "Quick, one more." They made another shake. As they tried to give it to Eddie, they saw his face: It was the school colors, purple and white. His eyes were popping like a frog's. His chest was heaving, burps were coming like a slow-motion machine gun. "Uh-oh," said Salami, "he's gonna do it. Let's get outta here!" They flung the glass into the sink and took off. At the door they met fellow nickelhead Tuna Casseroli coming in. Tuna, spotting one of his favorite victims, exclaimed, "Mini Mott!" He strode over to Eddie and without warning snatched him by the ankles and hoisted him upside down. "You heard of the bench press?" he called to Baloney and Salami. "Well, this is the Mott lift." He began raising and lowering Eddie and counting: "One . . . two . . . three . . ." The nickelheads screamed, "Tuna, DON'T!"

It was too late. Eddie began barfing at the high point of the lift, when his upside-down mouth was opposite Tuna's thighs. As Tuna, unaware of what was happening, lowered him, he spray-barfed Tuna's jeans from thigh to ankle, then slathered his sneakers.

Not wanting to be accomplices to murder, Baloney and Salami fled. Tuna stood frozen, beginning now to feel the warmth seeping through the denim. He held Eddie farther out from himself, as if the damage were not already done. When he finally gathered his courage to look down, he saw his victim's upside-down face, featuring the tiny twin pipes of his nostrils, and his own feet — or at least he assumed his feet were there, for nothing of his sneakers showed above the barf but two plastic lace tips. For some reason Eddie thought of a promotion Little Caesar's Pizza was running: "Extra Topping No Extra Charge."

To Eddie's amazement, the next voice was not Tuna's but someone else's, a man's deep voice booming: "Let him down easy, nosepicker."

15

Eddie swung his upside-down head past Tuna's pant leg. It was Bobo! Holding the cigar butt in his hand and advancing. "You got to the count of one, nosepicker."

Tuna let Eddie down, Bobo helped Eddie gather up his stuff, and they left. The last thing Eddie heard was the *squush-squush* of Tuna trying to walk.

In the hallway Bobo cupped Eddie's chin in one meaty paw. "You look sick. What was going on in there?"

"I'm okay now," said Eddie, "just weak. I think I lost about ten pounds of mass back there."

Cries of "Yo, Bobo!" erupted from students rushing for homeroom.

Eddie felt a sob coming on. The ordeal, the rescue, had left him drained of everything but an urge to hug the bus driver walking beside him and tear out into that big belly. He heard Bobo's gravelly voice say, "You better get goin' where you're supposed to go."

The hall was empty. Quickly, Eddie pressed his forehead into the belly (now, *that* was massive), whispered "Thanks," and ran off. Two rooms down he stopped, turned. "Hey, Bobo, what are you doing here, anyway?"

The cigar butt shifted in Bobo's mouth. "Late Room."

Eddie laughed at the joke and ran on.

As Eddie soon found out, it was no joke. Detention Room was in the same place as Late Room, and when he reported for his detention, sure enough, there was Bobo sitting in the front row.

"I thought you were kidding," said Eddie.

"I don't kid, kid," growled the bus driver.

Late- and Detention-Room monitors changed every week. This week it happened to be Miss Billups. "Eddie Mott?" she said. "Mr. Brimlow said the students on the bus did not have to come to Late Room. Only the driver."

Eddie cleared his throat and swallowed a few times. "I'm not here for Late Room."

Surprise showed on the teacher's face. Eddie Mott was not known as a troublemaker. "You're not? Are you on the detention list? I haven't even looked." She rummaged around the desk till she found the list. She looked from the paper to him.

"You are." She still didn't sound convinced. "May I ask what brings you here?"

Before Eddie could form an answer, Pickles, Salem, and Sunny entered the room. Miss Billups looked back at the detention sheet. "Now, you three definitely are not on the list."

"No, we're not," said Salem. "We're just here to give moral support to Eddie. It's his first-ever detention, and we thought maybe we could help him get through it."

"There's no rule against volunteering for detention, is there?" said Pickles.

Miss Billups chuckled. "No, I guess not. But I'd still like to find out why Mr. Mott's name is on this." She waved the sheet at them.

Sunny answered without hesitation. "He burped."

The teacher blinked. "He burped?"

"Big time."

"Big time?"

"He burped all over school, all day. He was grossing out teachers left and right. The last straw was in English class. He said, "Quoth the Raven . . . *Brrraawwwpp!*' Miss O'Malley told him, 'Edward Mott, you are the most disgusting, revolting, sickening student I have ever had in my life. You are grosser than — ' "

Eddie yelped, "She didn't say that!"

Miss Billups nodded with a faint smile. "I know. Why don't you just write 'I will mind my manners

68

in class' fifty times on the blackboard, and then you may go."

Pickles turned to Bobo. "Shouldn't you be out in your bus?"

Bobo turned his seat sideways and put his feet up on another desk. "I got late bus today."

"I don't believe you're really here."

"What do I look like, a mirage?"

"I don't believe you're really listening to Mr. Brimlow."

"That's life, kid. Some people you listen to, the rest you kick in the shins."

"The rest *you* kick in the shins," amended Miss Billups.

"You really think they would fire you?" said Sunny.

"Sure," said Bobo. "If they had more people wanted to be drivers, I'da been gone long ago." He flapped his hand. "*Sayonara.*"

"What's that mean?" said Eddie.

"It means good-bye in Japanese," said Salem.

Eddie's eyes bulged. "You speak Japanese?"

"Mr. Mott," said Miss Billups, "if you don't get up to the blackboard this minute, your penance will be doubled."

"What does penance mean?"

"Mr. Mott!"

Eddie went to the blackboard and began writing his fifty sentences — and so did Pickles, Sunny, and Salem.

For a minute Miss Billups just gaped at them: four students, backs to the classroom, all writing the same sentence over and over. "What," she said at last, "are you doing?"

"We're just supporting Eddie," said Pickles, continuing to write.

"Even though he's a criminal," said Sunny, whose sentences were the sloppiest.

Miss Billups just stared at them. Something good is happening here, she thought, something we don't teach them in school. The only sounds were the scrapes and squeaks of four pieces of chalk.

16

"Was I dreaming back there?" said Pickles.

"He didn't really say that, did he?" said Sunny.

"Yeah, he did," said Eddie.

Since the picklebus had been left home this day, the pickle posse was walking. After completing their sentences — all 200 of them — they had cleaned the blackboards and were bidding good-bye to Miss Billups when Bobo spoke up: "How'd you like a baby-sitting job?"

The four of them had simply stopped at the doorway and gawked. He went on to explain that he could never go anywhere because he could not find anyone to baby-sit for his three little ones. (*No kidding*, Sunny had thought.) Now he was thinking that the four of them together could do it. Pickles had said they would have to think about it.

At the end of the school driveway, they turned for home. "Do you believe him?" said Pickles.

"I don't," said Sunny.

"Neither do I," said Salem.

"I do," said Eddie.

"It's not like him," said Salem.

"Why should he give us a job?" said Sunny. "He hates kids."

"He doesn't hate kids," said Eddie. "And he said he would probably pay us good."

"Maybe it's a trick," said Pickles.

"Yeah," said Sunny. "He's trying to lure us into his house so he can murder us."

"No, he's not," said Eddie firmly. "He likes us."

Sunny finger-flicked the back of Eddie's head. "Who made you the big Bobo expert all of a sudden?"

"I did," said Eddie primly, and he told them the whole story of his adventures in the boys' room.

"Gosh," was all Salem could say.

"He saved your life," said Pickles.

Sunny said nothing.

They walked on.

Salem cleared her throat and said, as casually as possible, "Anybody ever hear of an Alan Kent?"

"Not me," said Pickles.

"He go to our school?" said Eddie.

"I really don't know," Salem nonchalantly lied.

Sunny plucked off Salem's black, floppy hat and plunked it on her own head. "What's this, you got the hots for this kid or something?" She scrutinized Salem, mischief in her eyes. "Is *that* why you weren't around for lunch today?"

Salem felt her cheeks burning. She snatched back her hat, and laughed. "Right. Do I look like a *hots* type of person?"

Before she sank any deeper, Pickles unwittingly saved her. He suddenly darted into the middle of the street. "Where's the snow?" he barked. He lifted his face to the sky and threw out his arms. "I . . . WANT . . . SNOW!'

The others were stunned. Normally Pickles was the coolest of them all.

"He's bumped his pumpkin," said Sunny.

Eddie jumped from the curb. "Hey, I have an idea. I got it from Pickles there, the way he's standing. You heard of a rain dance? Let's have — "

Salem finished it: "A *snow* dance!"

A car beeped; Pickles came back nodding. "Yeah . . . why not?"

"Let's go to the library," said Salem.

"And look up rain dancing," said Eddie.

"And change it to snow dancing!" said Pickles.

They started off walking; soon they were running.

The library had plenty of material on rain, but not much on rain dancing. Most helpful were pictures from the vertical file. They generally showed natives wearing skimpy costumes and masks, dancing under cloudless skies in various desert areas of the globe.

"You can't tell what the dance is like," said Pickles.

"All you can see is one step."

"We need movies," said Eddie.

They checked the video section, especially the *National Geographic* tapes. Nothing.

"We'll make our own dance," said Salem.

"Good idea," said Sunny. She did some swooping turns and elaborate arm movements.

"Snow does not listen to kung fu," said Salem.

"That's for the snow to decide," said Sunny and went off to section 796.815: Martial Arts.

Pickles continued to look through such subjects as Rain and Dance and Snow and Weather. Eddie looked into Bulk Up and Weight and Muscles and, when he was sure no one was looking, Hunk.

Salem headed for a special section in Reference. In this section the public library kept the yearbooks of each school in town. Since Plumstead was a brand-new middle school this year, it had no yearbook yet. The other middle school was Cedar Grove. When Plumstead opened, many Cedar Grove students were transferred there. Salem pulled last year's Cedar Grove yearbook off the shelf.

And hit paydirt.

There, among the seventh-grade class, was a

74

boy identified as Alan Kent. That made him an eighth-grader now. He had light-brown hair, a friendly smile. Could that face have written the love line question: "Be my valentine?"? Yes, she decided, he most certainly could have.

She went through the whole yearbook, searching for more of Alan Kent. He was in the school chorus and was a member of the Students for Earth Day committee. Even the grade schools had modest yearbooks. She found him in Drumore Elementary, Sunny's old school.

She dropped a dime in the copier and made a copy of his Cedar Grove picture. Best ten cents she'd ever spent. She put the picture in her book bag, then took it out. She couldn't stop looking at it.

She wandered among the stacks, trying to digest it all. An *eighth-grader*! Most eighth-grade boys didn't know sixth-grade girls existed. But of course, Alan Kent was no ordinary eighth-grade boy. Salem could see that already. He must be a strong and confident person, she thought, comfortable with himself and not afraid of his classmates ribbing him for "robbing the cradle." He's the type of person who sets a course and never strays from it, regardless of public pressure.

And that, Salem happily realized, was a description of herself as well. No wonder, when he cast his eyes over the student body, that he singled out the elegant girl with the long, brown hair,

Salem Brownmiller, whose maturity belied her age. Already she could feel herself bonding with this extraordinary young man.

Be my valentine?

"Yes," Salem whispered, pressing her lips to the ink-scented copy of his picture. "Yes, Alan, yes — "

At that moment — *POW!* — something walloped her in the forehead and sent her staggering back into Biography. As her senses cleared, she saw Sunny rushing, alarm in her eyes and a giggle in her voice. "Salem, I'm sorry. I was practicing my high kick." Sunny stood before her in stocking feet, an open book in one hand, the other reaching, touching her forehead. "Are you okay?"

Salem blew hair from her eyes. She glared. "Sure. Feel free to kick me any time."

Truth be told, Salem was barely annoyed. She had felt no pain from the kick, only force, and that was piddling. After all, what was a kick in the head compared to Cupid's arrow in the heart?

17

Salem was in the middle of math homework that night when the phone rang. It was Sunny. "He's in eighth grade, he's on Hi-Q, and he's in Homeroom 221."

Salem pretended ignorance. "What are you talking about? Who?"

"Okay, play dumb. AK. Ring a bell?"

AK. She knew. She saw the Love Line.

Salem's heart was racing. She could not speak. She heard Sunny's voice saying, "I felt bad about kicking you today, even if it *was* an accident, so I thought I'd do you a favor and find out more about AK. So I made a couple of phone calls. He's supposed to be shy, too."

Shy. Yes, that seemed right. Shyness could be so adorable in a boy. And Hi-Q, meaning he represented Plumstead in *Jeopardy*-like competitions with other schools. Meaning he was smart. It figured. Smart people seek each other out. Salem had intended to try out for the Hi-Q team next year.

"You're not talking," said Sunny.

"I know."

Sunny snickered, "It *could* be Avery Kribble, you know."

"God forbid!" yelped Salem, and all her pent-up emotions burst forth in loud, almost hysterical laughter. Sunny joined in.

"Mrs. Salem Kribble!" Sunny shrieked, and they howled some more.

The laughter lapsed into more silence, which became increasingly awkward. Finally Salem braced herself and said, "You won't go around saying anything, will you?"

"No," came the simple, prompt reply.

"Not even to Pickles and Eddie."

"Don't worry."

More silence. Then: "Sal?"

Salem winced. Rarely did Sunny call her Sal. When she did, it was usually because Salem was vulnerable. And suddenly Salem knew: Sunny was considering whether or not to point out that there were other SB's in school. Salem replied, "Yes?" as she silently prayed: *Don't say it, Sunny. Please don't.*

She didn't. "Nothing," she said. "Gotta go. Good luck. 'Bye." She hung up.

Salem laid down the receiver, but she kept her hand on it for a long time.

18

Homeroom 221 was at the far end of the second floor. After telling Pickles not to pick her up next morning, Salem arrived at 221 with exactly thirteen minutes before last bell.

On one side of 221 was the stairway to the first floor. On the other side was a water fountain. Salem spent a good two thirds of forever trying to appear inconspicuous as she strolled back and forth between stairway and fountain.

He wasn't there, and he wasn't there, and suddenly he was, seconds before last bell, racing up the stairs two — no, three — at a time, so fast that he was past her before she recognized him. He was bigger-looking than his seventh-grade picture and with longer hair and so much more real than copy toner and paper. His mad dash up the stairs identified him as a last-minute arriver and a real go-getter. Salem was liking him more and more. He flew into 221 as she ran to her own homeroom, more from excitement than fear of being late, which she was.

She watched for him in the hallways between classes. It wasn't until after fourth period that she spotted him, heading her way, talking to another boy, part of the mob. She wondered how many times he had spotted her in the hallways, followed her with his eyes, felt the feeling that became the thought that became the question in Love Lines.

Another two inches and they would have brushed shoulders. He breezed on by, talking to his friend. Did he see her? His eyes seemed to sweep over her, as they swept over the hallway, the mob — but did he *see* her? Did his eyes, for an atomized instant, land on her? Yes, she thought. No, she thought.

"He's supposed to be shy," Sunny had said.

Salem was useless the rest of the day.

At dismissal she raced upstairs, three at a time as he had. He was at his locker, shuffling books, fooling around, taking forever. Fast before school, slow after. She liked that. She lingered at a distance. At last he closed the locker and headed down the stairs. She followed. She hoped he was going home. She was about to find out where Alan Kent lived.

One foot each on the picklebus, Pickles and Eddie waited for the girls after school. They were at the side door by the parking lot, the picklebus terminal.

"What's keeping them?" said Eddie.

"Beats me," said Pickles. "They say anything about being late?"

"Nope, not to me."

They waited.

Pickles pointed to a nearby tree. "Look."

Eddie looked. "What?"

"The tree."

"What about it?"

"The branches. The limbs."

"I'm *looking*."

"Buds."

Eddie squinted. "Those little nubbers?"

"Those little nubbers."

Eddie nodded. "Okay." He shrugged. "So?"

"So, buds are supposed to come in the spring. This is February. That shows you how warm it's been. The weather's all screwed up. It's even messing up the trees." He gazed upward. "Must be the ozone hole."

"What's that?"

"A hole in the atmosphere."

Eddie squinted into a sky that was brightly overcast, a high silken blanket. "I don't see a hole."

"You can't see it. Anyway, it's over the South Pole. But it's letting too much sun in, warming everything up."

"I like warm," said Eddie. "I don't like cold weather."

"It doesn't snow in warm weather."

"I know, but that's the *only* thing I like about cold weather — snow. I wish it could snow in the summer. That's what I'd like. Is there any place like that? I'd move there."

"Maybe Mars." Pickles scanned the students swarming out of school. "Still don't see them." He turned back to Eddie, grinned and whispered, "Moocho Malt."

Eddie shrieked and covered his ears. Since the three-glass, upside-down Tuna shake in the boys' room, he could not bear the sound or thought of those two words. He didn't do so well with "mayonnaise," "peanut butter," or "parsley" either.

Pickles laughed and pulled Eddie's hands away. "You can come out now. I won't do it anymore." He put his arm around Eddie. "You know, since you can't drink you-know-what anymore, we're going to have to bulk you up some other way."

Eddie nodded. "Yeah, like what?"

Pickles pointed to his head. "Your mind. I'm going to start reading up on hypnotism. I'll put you under" — he wiggled his fingers before Eddie's eyes — "and make you believe that skinny is beautiful."

Eddie was trying to figure out if his leg was being pulled when Pickles said, "There's Salem. Going out the front door. Let's go."

19

Oh no! Salem groaned when she saw them coming.

Eddie called, "Salem!"

Salem pretended not to hear and kept walking. Alan Kent was ten feet ahead of her, heading down the driveway in the midst of the raucous, horseplaying, homebound mob.

The picklebus pulled alongside her. "Come on, Salem," said Eddie, sliding back on the green surfboard to give her room in the middle, "hop on."

She wished Eddie would keep his voice down. "I think I'll walk today," she practically whispered. "I could use the exercise."

Eddie and Pickles yapped together: *"Exercise?"* Salem was widely known to be allergic to exercise. "Well, we'll just cruise close by then," said Pickles, "so we can pick you up and take you to the hospital when you collapse."

Salem wanted to kill them. "Don't bother," she gritted.

"No bother," Pickles said cheerily.

"Picklepeople forever," chimed Eddie.

They weren't going to vanish. Every passing second increased the risk that Alan Kent would overhear or turn and get the impression that she liked these two bozos. He was turning left at the end of the driveway, in the direction the picklebus would normally go.

She gave Alan Kent a departing look and snarled, "O-*kay* — but I want to go this way today." She pointed to the right. "I need a change of scenery."

"No problem," said Pickles. "Alllll aboard!"

She hopped on before he got any louder, and they pushed off.

"Where's Sunny?" Salem asked as they left the school behind.

Pickles shrugged. "That girl? Who knows what she's up to?"

Before long, they would all know.

The picklebus dropped Salem off at her house. At Pickles' house, his mother met them in the living room. "Sunny said to tell you she couldn't wait any longer. She'll see you tomorrow."

Pickles stared at her. "She was here?"

"In the basement. She said she was supposed to meet you there. You had something to show — "

Pickles was flying down the stairs, Eddie at his

heels. The basement light was still on. In the back corner the olive green tarp was on the floor. The pickleboggan was naked. As they approached, they saw a note taped to the green-painted side. It said, in Sunny Wyler's bold handwriting:

DON'T EVER TRY
TO KEEP A SECRET
FROM ME AGAIN!!!!!!
(ha-ha)

That evening, shortly after finishing dinner, Salem received a phone call. A strange, raspy voice croaked cryptically, "The main entrance to the school. Who will get there first? You . . . or the TV stations?" *Click*.

Salem was not good at mysteries. For several minutes the weird phone call meant absolutely nothing to her. Then, somehow, it did. What came to her at first was not knowledge, but a queasy, chilling, unarticulated feeling that she'd better get on over to that school — *pronto!*

She was not allowed out alone after dark, but there was no way she would ask her father to drive. It was only six o'clock. Running, she could make it in five minutes. She threw on a jacket and sneaked out the back door.

She knew by now that the voice had been Sunny's, disguised. As she ran, she kept hearing her own plea: "You won't go around saying anything, will you . . . will you . . . will you . . .?"

She ran faster.

The banner was visible from the sidewalk. She dragged herself and the sharp stitch in her side up the driveway. The banner was made of sheets of paper stapled together. It stretched across all four front doors, about fifteen feet. It said, in huge red letters:

SALEM BROWNMILLER LOVES
ALAN KENT

Gasping, she took it down. She slumped back down the driveway, dragging the banner behind. She stopped to gather it up. She folded it, pleating it neatly sheet by sheet. She would save it forever. She was almost — *almost* — glad that Sunny did it.

20

Sunny finished cutting the eyeholes and laid down the scissors. "Why am I doing this?"

"You're doing it to bring snow," said Salem.

"Get serious."

"You're doing it because you want to make up for the rotten trick you played on your best friend last night."

"Who's my best friend?"

"Don't be funny."

Sunny scoffed, "Rotten? You're not even close. I did it on Friday night, when nobody would be there for two days, didn't I? I called you, didn't I?"

"You promised you wouldn't say anything."

"I didn't. I wrote it. Try again."

Salem sighed mightily. "You're doing it because Pickles is desperate for snow, and you love him so you'll do anything to help him out. That's my last reason. If you don't like it, go home."

Sunny stood before Salem's mirror and held the

87

sheet in front of her, as though appraising a dress. "I don't love Pickles."

"Of course you do. Like you love Eddie and yours truly."

"Who's yours truly?"

"Me."

"I love kung fu, that's who I love." She did a left-leg side-high kick. "Hai-YAH!"

Salem flinched. "You know, Miss Wyler, you have a problem."

"That so?"

"Yes. You don't come to terms with your feelings. You — "

"Ah!" Sunny raised her finger. "But I do come to terms with *your* feelings."

"While you're giving me a heart attack. As I was saying, you can get away with it now, because you're a youngster. Plus, we understand you, we know that's how you are, we know you're not as heartless as you talk." She glared at Sunny. "Or *act*. But someday . . . someday you're going to meet somebody you like, but nothing will come of it because you don't know how to admit it."

Arms folded, Sunny waited for Salem to finish. Then she replied, in wincing disbelief, *"Youngster?* I never heard anybody under ninety use that word." She pronounced it again: *"Youngster."*

Salem sniffed, "I beg your pardon. I keep forgetting how *minuscule* your vocabulary is."

Sunny simpered, "Boo-hoo." She pulled the

88

sheet over herself, working the eyeholes into position. "I'm still waiting for some answer that makes sense. Why are you and I standing here in your bedroom with sheets over our heads?"

Salem sighed. "Okay, how about this? We don't really believe it's going to bring snow, or at least we're not sure. But mostly we're doing it because we're kids and it's Saturday and we're bored and it's something to do."

Sunny pointed, making her sheet tepee toward Salem. "Bingo."

The doorbell rang. "That's the guys," said Salem. "Let's go."

The two-eyed sheets floated down the stairway like a pair of parachutes.

Five minutes later Salem's backyard looked like a convention of ghosts. Pickles was the most elaborately done up, adding a mask to his plain white sheet. Made of papier-mâché, the mask resembled a pumpkin — a white pumpkin — with a grotesque slash for a mouth and monsterish eyes. Erupting from the top was a twelve-inch stack of bristles from a household broom, also painted white.

Sunny rapped on the mask. "Knock-knock."

Pickles' voice sounded slightly hollow. "Who's there?"

"Atch."

"Atch who?"

"*Gesundheit*. Knock-knock."

"Who's there?"

"Sunny."

"Sunny who?"

"Sunny and warm the rest of the winter. Not a flake of snow."

"Sunny," snapped Salem, "try to be a little serious for once in your life, will you?"

Sunny howled. "Serious? How can I be serious looking at him. He looks like Snow Broom Butt from Outer Space." She lurched about the yard, hooting ghostily, "Boooo . . . booooo." Then she sneaked up behind Eddie and lifted his sheet.

"Hey!" he yelped.

"Just wanted to see if you were wearing your Superman undies." She lurched away. "Boooo . . . boooo."

"She's outta control," said Eddie.

"Pickles," said Salem, "she didn't want to do this in the first place. Maybe it's better without her. She's only going to mess it up."

Silence within the white pumpkinoid. Then, in a voice with a gangsterish twang: "She's in the pickle posse, she stays in the pickle posse. The only way anybody leaves this gang is in a coffin."

Sunny raced to Pickles, fell at his feet. "Oh thank you, Great White Broom Butt. Thank you for keeping me. I'll make you proud." She skipped about the yard, squeaking like a tot, "I'm in the gang! I'm in the gang! I'm a little baby snowflake.

Now I melted and went to snowflake heaven. Now I'm a leeee-tle baby snowflake ghost. I don't say boo anymore, I say goo . . . goooo . . . goooo . . ."

There was no use fighting it. The other three sheets cracked up.

When they finally laughed themselves out over Sunny's antics, Pickles said, "Okay, can we get down to business now?"

As Pickles was saying this, Sunny circled around behind him. Salem and Eddie saw her remove her shoe, they saw her lift her sheet to her waist, they saw her take aim — and still they did not believe that she would do it.

She did.

With a ringing "Hai-YAH!" she snapped her right leg high; the heel of her foot caught Pickles' papier-mâché mask dead center. The mask split vertically in two from back to front. The eyes parted, the nose disappeared, the horrible mouth became two. All that held the mask together was the broom top, and when Sunny neatly plucked it out, the two halves fell to the ground like a cracked nutshell. The nut itself stood there for a full minute, shook his head in disgust, said, "I give up," yanked off his sheet, and stomped away.

"Party pooper Pickles," Sunny called.

Salem chuckled, "Hey, try saying that five times fast."

For the next minute Salem's backyard resounded to sounds most curious: "Party pooper pickles. Party pooper pickles. Party pipper pickles. Party pooper pickers. Perty popple pickles. Pookle perpy pittles. Picky packer pooples. Pocker pooker picker . . ."

Pickles, who had stopped at the driveway, turned slowly, hands on hips. "I hope you all have sleds of your own — "

"Pickle packle peekle," said Sunny.

"Pooter poopy doopy," said Eddie.

" — because when it snows I'll be going up to Heller's Hill by myself."

"Poofles," said Sunny.

"Poo," said Eddie.

Pickles sagged. He slumped to a seat in the driveway. He looked at himself — the sheet slung over his shoulder, half a snow dance mask in each hand. He wanted to cry, he really did.

21

Salem knew Miss Billups was talking to the class, and she knew she ought to be paying attention, but how could she, with Alan Kent somewhere in the same building — the same town — the same planet? Salem had written of love in a few of her stories, but she'd had no idea it could be this powerful, this all-consuming.

And frustrating.

She was beginning to understand how well earned was Alan's reputation for shyness. Again this morning, she had passed him in the hall, and again he had failed to acknowledge her. Which was not to say he did not see her. She felt certain this time that he had. For a good three or four seconds, he was unmistakably looking her way. Apparently, not even his shyness could prevent a deeper, primal urge to feast his eyes upon her. But then he looked away and, as before, went on walking and talking by. No smile, no nod, nothing.

Maybe it wasn't shyness, maybe it was self-discipline. Maybe, while his heart was saying, "Go get her," his head was saying, "You're not ready for women yet." Or maybe he was unsure of her. Maybe he was afraid that she, a mere sixth-grader, would simply laugh or blubber if he made his move.

Maybe, maybe.

Salem was getting fed up with maybes. There was no maybe about her answer to Alan's big question. The answer was yes. Yes, Alan, I *will* be your valentine. She wanted to shout it in his face, shout it over the PA system, shout it from the top of the bleachers on the football field. YES!

And Valentine's Day itself, February 14, was Thursday, only three days away. Valentine's Day was not a day for maybes, for questions, for suspense. It was a day when matters became settled, a day for answers, for yesses. A day for — she shivered at the very thought of the word — *couples*. Would Thursday dawn to find Salem Brownmiller and Alan Kent a couple? To think so made her want to giggle and squeal like a second-grader.

What a crime, what a stupid and senseless crime it would be if Valentine's Day came and went and still nothing was settled. Well, that wasn't going to happen, not if Salem could help it. She had to break through this barrier between them. She did not care to give her answer to someone who was afraid to say hello to her. She was a female. She was supposed to have feminine wiles. What was she waiting for? Use them! If he was having a hard time approaching her, she would make it easier. She would make herself impossible to miss.

"Well, it looks like you got your wish," Sunny said to her as they walked out of class.

Salem blinked, stared at Sunny. "Huh? What wish?"

"The big George Washington camp-out," said Pickles.

Eddie snapped his fingers in front of her face. "Hey, are you here?"

Salem stared at them all. She smiled weakly. "Now I am. I guess I wasn't listening in class. I was doing my, uh, math homework."

"Yeah," snickered Sunny, "one plus one equals two."

Salem shot her a look.

"Everybody has to do a project," said Pickles. "You're allowed to go together, up to four to a team."

"It can be almost anything," said Eddie, "as long as it has to do with that winter at Valley Forge."

"So we figured we might as well do your bone

soup thing," said Pickles. "How about this Saturday night? My backyard."

"I'll bring the tent," said Sunny.

"I'll bring firewood," said Eddie.

"I'll bring the pot," said Pickles.

Everyone turned grinning to Salem. She rolled her eyes. "O-*kay*. I'll bring the bone."

That night, while plotting her strategy, Salem received a phone call.

"Hello," said a deep voice, "this is Alan Kent. I just want you to know that you are the most beautiful girl I ever saw and I hope some day you will become my wife."

"Hello, Sunny," said Salem.

"Eddie just called," said Sunny.

"So?"

"Pickles just called him."

"So?"

"Bobo just called him."

"Bobo? The bus driver?"

"Yeah."

"Why?"

"Remember he asked us that day if we would baby-sit for him?"

"Yeah."

"He's asking."

"What did Pickles tell him?"

"He told him no."

"Why?"

"It's for Saturday night."
"And that's the night we're camping out."
"Right."
"Okay."
"Okay. 'Bye."
" 'Bye."

22

In the old days, or at least in the old stories and movies, when a lady wished to attract the attention of a gentleman, she would drop an embroidered hanky as she was strolling through the park, preferably with a parasol. Whereupon the gentleman would gallantly retrieve the hanky from the ground and call, "Ma'am!" The lady would stop, the parasol would swing, she would turn just enough and say sweetly, innocently, "Yes?" He would not say it then; first he would walk briskly to her, and then he would say it: "You dropped something." And she would say, eyes all wide and innocent, "Well my, my, so I did," or simply, "Why, thank you." And then he would return the hanky to her, preferably passing it under his nose, for the hanky would be perfumed, and their fingers would touch for a moment, and their eyes would more than touch, and he would smile and nod and say "Charmed," and she would smile and the parasol would begin to slowly spin and they would live happily ever after.

Back then, every day was Valentine's Day.

Well, there was no park and no parasol, but also no reason why the old wile couldn't work. And so Salem had stationed herself on the stairway landing outside Room 221 just after the doors opened on Tuesday morning. All the ingredients were here, just brought up to date. Instead of a park, there was Plumstead Middle School. Instead of an embroidered hanky, a black, floppy felt hat.

The minutes and the students went by; the gabble and rush of opening bell. She waited, hat in hand, growing increasingly nervous as the time neared 7:48 and the student flood became a trickle. She half expected him to be late, as before, and he was. The stairwell was an echoing hollow below her when a loud thump signaled that the first floor's swinging door had been slammed open. Foot sounds followed, at intervals indicating at least three steps at a time — and there he was, book bag flapping wildly, careening through the turn at the mid-stair landing, heading straight for her now, head down, pounding the steps, panting . . .

She dropped her hat. She dropped it on the top step, in the middle, directly in his path. He couldn't possibly miss it. And he didn't. He ran right over it, planted his right foot smack on top of it, kept on going, burst through the door, and was into his homeroom.

Salem stared at her hat, or was that her heart lying there? She picked it up. A dusting of light brown showed where his foot had landed. She was about to brush it off when she remembered whose sneaker the dust had come from. She slipped the hat into her book bag. The bell rang. This time she did not run.

23

By the end of first period, she had it figured out. He didn't mean to step on her hat. He was going so fast, he didn't even see it. Or if he did, it was just a black blur on the step as he flew by. In any case, he certainly did not know he was stepping on his Love Line person's hat.

She felt better. And ready for another try.

They were scheduled to make their daily hallway pass-by after fourth period. This time she would drop the passive, little lady role. Since he was afraid to make a move, she would make it for him. She would speak. She would say "Hi" to him. Maybe "Hi, Alan." With a big smile. And with a look in her eyes that would answer his question, that would say, *Yes, I will be your valentine.*

When the bell ended fourth period, she was first out the door. She was racing to the spot where they usually passed, in front of the Science Lab, when she realized that if she outraced her usual pace, she might miss him. So she slowed down.

She kept to the middle of the hall, so she could move to either side to pass closely by him.

And here he came, gabbing away as usual with his after-fourth-period friend. She took a deep breath, she put on her best smile, she put the *Yes* in her eyes, the valentine in her voice: "Hi, Alan."

He stopped talking. His eyes darted about the mob. His head swung to one side, then the other. He smiled — the first time she had ever seen him smile in person, the most wonderful smile — and said, "Hi" — to the girl walking behind her.

By afternoon she had it figured. The hall was just too crowded. He hadn't seen her coming. All he heard was a voice in the mob. How was he to know which of those dozens of girls' faces passing by was the one who spoke his name? He just happened to pick out the wrong one, that's all.

It was time for a new approach. She would have to isolate him, one on one. At his locker after school. When there would be no rush, no confounding mob. No more messing around, no wiles, no excuses, no shyness. Just him and her and the answer to a question.

After school she waited by the water fountain outside Room 221. She watched the students come out, visit their lockers, drift, or dash away. He didn't come out. The hallway was deserted. The teacher came out and walked past her down the blue-carpeted avenue.

Salem peeked inside the room. Empty. On the way out, she stopped by the office to check the bulletin board. There was a Hi-Q meet today, at Tarrytown Middle School. The team bus had left after sixth period. He hadn't been in school for over an hour.

Sunny called that night.

"Where you been?"

Salem did not reply.

"I said — "

"I heard what you said."

"So answer the question."

"There you go again."

"There I go what?"

"That tone of voice."

"Huh?"

"I do not respond to questions that are growled at me like commands."

Sunny paused. "What are you so touchy about all of a sudden?" There was no answer. "As if I didn't know."

"What's that supposed to mean?"

"AK. That's what it means. It means you're all wrapped up in this stupid eighth-grader like you're twenty-one years old or something and you don't ride home on the picklebus anymore and you don't have time for your friends anymore because you're being a lovesick jerk, that's what — "

Click. Salem hung up.

Five seconds later the phone rang again. Salem picked it up.

" — it means. And anyway that's not even why I called, which I half wish I hadn't now, but I'm supposed to tell you. Bobo wants us to baby-sit so bad that he said we can do the camp-out in his yard Saturday night and watch the three monsters at the same time. So Pickles told him okay. So you still bring the bone. Oh, excuse me, there I go growling at you again. How's this? If you please, Miss Brownmiller, you are requested to be in the company of a bone when you attend the activities Saturday night. A bone from your own body will do nicely." *Click*.

24

First thing Wednesday morning Salem headed for Room 221, but this time she wasn't going to hang around. No waiting by the water fountain or lingering on the landing. What she had to do would take only a second.

The night before, she had hatched a new plan. She would cut right to the heart of the matter. She would answer his Love Line question, not with her eyes, but directly, unmistakably. In writing. She could have kicked herself for not thinking of it before. She was a writer, and here was the perfect chance to show her stuff.

She started composing at eight o'clock. By the time she finished polishing the final draft, it was almost eleven. It wasn't long, but it was perfect.

> *Dear Alan,*
>   *Your question still echoes in my*
> *heart: "Be my valentine?"*

*When I think of the shyness you
had to overcome in order to write
that, I perceive the depths of your
feeling.*

*When I think of your courage to face
the mocking mobs who would laugh
and say, "She's too young!" I feel the
presence of true love.*

*Be shy no more, dearest Alan. Fear
not, for the answer is a resounding
YES! YES! YES!*

> *Your valentine,*
> *Salem*
> *(SB)*

She had sprayed two puffs of her mother's perfume on the note, put it in a small envelope, sealed it, and placed it under her pillow and slept on it. And now as she approached his locker, she drew it from her pocket. A girl went to a nearby locker. Salem detoured to the water fountain. When the girl left, she glanced around, saw the coast was clear, rushed to his locker, and slipped the envelope into the crack at the bottom of the locker door. It wouldn't go through. Too thick. Loud voices echoed in the stairwell — kids were coming. She emitted a strangled screech. She tore off the envelope, she unfolded the note. It couldn't get any thinner. Footsteps pounded the stairs. Shouts, laughter. *Fit*, she prayed, *please fit*. She slipped it in. It went. The door thumped open. She ran.

The next day and a half were the longest in Salem's life. She learned what they meant in novels about the pain of waiting. She could not eat, she could not sleep, she could not concentrate. She could only wait, a helpless hostage of time. She had never wanted to understand Patrick Wister this well.

When she passed Alan in the hall after fourth period that day, she made no attempt to attract his attention. She did, however, study him closely as he passed. If a boy received a note in his locker, could you tell just by looking at him later in the hall? She imagined it might show in his eyes. They might be wandering over the crowd, anxiously, even desperately, scanning the faces, seeking that special one. But he was looking only at his hallway buddy, gabbing away with him as usual.

Maybe, she thought, considering how rushed he was each morning, he hadn't even seen it yet.

After school, she stayed away from 221. She lingered just inside the main door, where he would pass on his way home. Maybe he was just now visiting his locker for the first time today. Maybe he was just now noticing the note. She tried to picture it: He unlocks the lock, opens the door. He's reaching for books or whatever when, suddenly, he sees it. Maybe he doesn't even realize what it is at first, maybe he assumes it's just a loose sheet of his own paper. He's about to close the locker when — *ah!* — he gets a whiff of the perfume. Now where could that enchanting scent be coming from? That piece of paper? He picks it up, sniffs it. His senses drown in a confusion of ecstasy. (Thank you, Mother.) At last he opens his eyes and — yes, *now* — he reads the note.

Just thinking about it in the doorway, Salem began to tremble and sweat. Oh great, she thought, he finally comes to me and I'm a shaking, soggy, smelly mess. She brought herself under control. She thought of other, calmer things.

It was critical that she make herself available to him now at every possible moment. The worst thing that could happen would be for him to read the note and to come looking for her and — she shuddered at the thought — *not* be able to find her.

And so she waited and waited in the doorway. She knew her picklepals would once again be waiting for her in vain, and she did feel bad about that. They simply would not understand that matters of the heart override all else. She would make it up to them Saturday night.

It was as if her heart saw him first, for it seemed to quicken a split second before her eyes found him in the crowd passing the glass tank that housed Humphrey the hamster, the school mascot. He was passing the office now, now the student art display, in the midst of the departing mob, chatting with a girl . . . a brown-haired girl . . . chatting and laughing, passing by now, right in front of her — how could he not see her? — and through the doorway and out into the sunshine, still laughing as they buttoned up their jackets because the weather had finally turned cold. The girl was much taller than Salem, obviously an eighth-grader. Her eyelashes, as they had passed, seemed a foot long. They did not part outside the building. They did not go to separate buses. Salem stepped outside and watched them walk down the long driveway, bobbing into and out of view among the surging students. They did not separate at the end of the driveway, but both turned to the left and walked up the sidewalk.

Together.

The rest of that day and night was a nightmare from which Salem could not awaken.

Was the girl a friend — or *girl*friend? How could it be that Salem presented herself to Alan over three days, and not once did he speak to her, or nod, or smile? Just how shy could a shy person possibly be? Or how wrong? Had there been a horrible mistake? Was someone else AK? Avery Kribble? No. That was as laughable, as unthinkable as ever. AK *had* to be Alan Kent. So then:

SB. Did SB *have* to be Salem Brownmiller? Maybe the girl with short brown hair and foot-long eyelashes was an SB. Or maybe she was just a friend. He was allowed to have friends who happened to be girls, wasn't he?

Wasn't he?

25

February 14.

Salem stood at her bedroom window, one sock on, one in hand. The sun humped reddish over the horizon like one lobe of a heavenly valentine. Her plan had been to wait as long as necessary for a response to her note. That was no longer possible. Suspense was blowing her up like a balloon. If she didn't do something quick, she would pop.

Forty minutes later she stood by the stairway leading to Room 221 — not at the top, but at the bottom. She did not walk back and forth, she did not pretend she was doing something else. She simply planted herself in front of the bottom step and waited. Whatever happened, one thing was certain: He was not going to miss her this time.

She had rehearsed her part a hundred times, but now she could remember nothing but the first two words, which bolted on their own from her mouth as he came suddenly bursting through the door: "Alan, stop!" She scrunched her shoulders and shut her eyes, waiting for him to bowl her over. When she dared to peek, she was staring into his neck. Had he seemed this much taller than her before? The abrupt halting of his momentum had left him tilted forward, looming almost directly above her head. She could smell the banana he had had for breakfast, probably during his mad dash to school.

In her romantic ruminations, she had never considered being this physically close to a boy. It was a little scary. She tried to back up, but her heel bonked into the bottom step. She ran her heel up the vertical to the lip, then lifted herself onto the step. She was now looking directly into his eyes. They were blue. They were glaring at her. She turned away from them.

"What?" he said, not very pleasantly.

She could not think.

He spoke again, his irritation plainly showing. "Wha'd you stop me for?" He looked up the stairs. "The bell's gonna ring."

She took a deep breath. "Did you get my note?"

He looked baffled. "Huh?"

"The *note*. In your locker yesterday."

His expression went through a series of changes that she could not identify. He stepped back. For the moment he had forgotten the time. "Yeah?" He said it like a question.

"Well?"

"Well what?"

She wished he would leave the questions to her. "Well . . . what do you think?"

"About what?"

"The *note*." This was not how she had imagined the conversation going.

He took another step back. He cocked his head to one side. He squinted at her. "Did *you* write that?"

And suddenly, with chilling finality, from the way he said "you" and from the look on his face, she knew the truth. She knew she would never get to say the words.

The bell rang.

He jumped onto the step beside her. He looked down on her, down from a height of twenty feet, it seemed. He said, not unkindly, "What grade are you in?" He waited only a second, then dashed away.

She whispered to the empty stairway: "Sixth."

26

Everyone met at Bobo's house Saturday at five o'clock. Eddie brought the firewood, Sunny the tent, Salem the bone, and Pickles the pot. Everyone but Pickles was taxied to the house by a parent. Pickles came on the long, green, six-wheeled bus. The pot hung from the handlebars; a patchwork quilt was tied to the floor.

Besides the firewood, Eddie arrived with five blankets, a sleeping bag, a pillow, a candy-striped ski cap, a ski mask, a first-aid kit, a flashlight, a Monopoly game, a twenty-six-inch Samsonite suitcase, and a whistle around his neck.

"Where do you think you're going?" Sunny squawked when she saw it all piled on Bobo's back porch. "Siberia?"

"It pays to be prepared," Eddie replied.

She tugged on the whistle. "What's this for?"

"In case we need to call for help."

Sunny wagged her head. Before Eddie could stop her, she unzipped the suitcase. "Oh no!" she

114

cried and pulled out a roll of toilet paper. Just then Bobo came onto the porch. Sunny waved the roll in his face. "It looks like Eddie Mott has plans for your backyard."

Bobo pointed to Eddie, who snatched the roll back. "You take a poop in my backyard," he growled, "and it's the last poop you'll ever take."

Bobo nodded at the tent. "You better put that thing up before it gets dark. I'll keep the monsters inside till I go."

"Can't you take them with you?" Sunny pleaded.

"Then who are you gonna baby-sit?" said Bobo.

"Eddie!" Sunny yipped. Eddie bounced the toilet paper off Sunny's head, everyone laughed, and Pickles dragged the tent into the yard.

The tent was raised and staked by nightfall, thanks mainly to Pickles. As he worked and directed the others, he kept saying, "Feels like snow . . . feels like snow."

Indeed, the temperature had been February-cold for several days, and overcast since Friday. There was no moonlight, and the night air was dense and still and utterly silent, as if waiting.

Pickles never stopped moving, now hammering a stake, now laying the canvas floor of the tent, now starting up a fire in the spot Bobo had designated. Repeating, almost singing, "Feels like snow," he bounced from chore to chore, as if by sheer activity he might persuade snow to fall.

In the meantime, Sunny kept herself and everyone else amused. For the most part she picked on Eddie. He constantly had to chase her from his belongings, as she insisted that if she were allowed a full search, sooner or later she would uncover a teddy bear.

Salem, by way of her mother's friendship with a butcher, had brought a huge shank bone from, it seemed, an apatosaurus. In Sunny's hands it became everything from a Continental soldier's drill musket to a twirler's baton to a flailing, whipsawing, martial-arts weapon.

Salem tried. She really tried to hang onto the devastation that had overwhelmed her at the foot of the stairwell Thursday morning. It seemed as if she had passed through the whole history of love in one week, and all she had to show for it was a flat, clobbered feeling. But at least it was a reminder of romance, and in a perverse sort of way she wanted to hang onto it.

But Sunny was making it awfully hard. Sunny kept poking her in the ribs with the bone. In time Salem began to suspect that Sunny guessed what had happened and was determined not to let her best friend feel sorry for herself. By the time "Michael Jordan" dunked the bone into the pot of boiling water and went into her cackling witch routine, Salem was laughing loudest of all.

Shortly before seven, with earsplitting shrieks, the three little monsters were let loose into the backyard. Bobo called from the porch: "I'll be back around eleven. Have a nice time!" He laughed and was gone.

From the start, the Bobo kids drove the baby-sitters batty. As soon as they discovered the sleeping bags, all three squeezed into one and went rolling about the yard like a giant worm. Then each climbed into a bag of his own, and they played bedroll demolition derby.

They found the toilet paper. Five minutes later a mummy stood where Eddie had been.

When they discovered the name of the baby-sitter with the green sneakers, they brought a jar of finger pickles from the refrigerator and had a finger pickle fight.

They kept trying to take the bone from the boiling water, but it was too hot. So they made the fire even hotter by feeding it the paper money from Eddie's Monopoly game.

And of course, when they discovered the picklebus, the Bobo kids, whose names were Wayne, Mookie, and Bert, went totally gonzo. Sunny, Salem, and Eddie had to forcibly wrench them away as Pickles parked the bus around the front of the house.

At that point the baby-sitters figured they'd better start saying no.

"Wanna see my boogie collection?"

"No."

"Can I cut a window in the tent?"

"No."

"Can I put Mookie's gerbil in the blender?"

"No!"

It was an avalanche of no's. So when Wayne had his next idea, he didn't even bother to ask. He just sneaked into the house and did it. When Sunny went looking, she found him dragging his mattress down the stairway.

"What are you doing!" she screeched.

"We're camping out, ain't we?" he said. "I'm bringing my bed."

Sunny yelled for Pickles, and together they lugged the mattress back upstairs. As they lifted it onto the box spring, they heard a whirring noise below. They stared at each other. *"Blender!"*

In the kitchen they found Wayne standing on a chair, a devilish grin on his face and a small, brown animal, presumably Mookie's gerbil, in his hand. He was dangling it over the buzzing blender.

At that moment Eddie came in the back door, saw what was happening and yelled, "Drop it!"

"No!" roared Pickles. *"Don't* drop it!" and he jerked the blender cord from its socket. The whirring blur became silvery blades, spinning, slowing, stopped.

"I'm calling your father," said Sunny.

"You're no fun," grumbled Wayne as Pickles confiscated the gerbil. "You don't let us do nothin'. I want Sally back."

"Sally?" said Sunny. "Who's that?"

"Our reg'lar baby-sitter, that's who. And I'm telling her on you!"

"Fine," said Sunny. "I'll tell your father to send her over. I'm resigning. Pick, give me that paper."

Pickles pulled a scrap of paper from his pocket and handed it over. Bobo had told them he was going to the Moose Lodge to play bingo. He had written the phone number on the paper.

Sunny called from the dining room. The phone rang a long time before some man — or moose — answered. While he went off to get Bobo, Sunny heard music in the background. Didn't sound like bingo.

At last Bobo came on the line. "They burn the house down yet?"

"Everything but," said Sunny. "Wayne tried to blender the gerbil."

The phone in her hand laughed for a full minute. "He just does that to get a rise outta ya. He wouldn't really do it. He loves that varmint. He played that once on me, too."

"Did he do it to Sally?"

Silence. "Who?"

"Sally? The regular baby-sitter?"

"Oh, Sally. Uh, sure, yeah, her, too. So that's all, huh? Gotta get back to bingo. Have a nice night."

He hung up before Sunny could resign.

"What did he say?" said Pickles.

"Have a nice night." She put up the receiver. "He didn't sound like himself."

"What do you mean?"

Sunny shrugged. "I don't know. He was laughing. He sounded, like, in a good mood."

Pickles frowned. "You sure it was Bobo?"

Outside again, Wayne broke open a stick of bubblegum, then tossed the wrapper into the soup. He stared at the baby-sitters, daring them to object. "Let him go," Pickles told the others. "We're not going to eat it anyway."

That was all Wayne, Mookie, and Bert had to hear. In short order, the bone and bubblegum wrapper were joined by a clump of grass, a brick, a cicada shell, a rusty screwdriver, a Dr Pepper can, a handful of stones, and a stiff, shriveled, long-dead earthworm. All of this was accompanied by loud and rising merriment, at the height of which Mookie fell onto his back, pulled off his shoes and socks, and flipped the socks into the pot.

"Sock soup!" shrieked Wayne, and even the baby-sitters had to laugh.

Salem took pictures then, to go along with the written report they had to submit for the project, or what was left of it. Naturally, the little ones wanted their pictures taken, so Salem did them first. Then she shooed them off and snapped another dozen photos of the tent, the pot and fire, her fellow "soldiers."

It was several minutes after the photo session when Eddie said, "Hey, it's quiet."

They glanced around.

"Must be in the tent," said Sunny. She looked. "Nope."

Already Pickles was heading toward the back porch. He disappeared into the shadows beside the house. Several seconds later they heard his cry from the front: "The picklebus is gone!"

27

They clustered out front under the cold, dim glow of the streetlight. Pickles put his finger to his lips. "Listen."

Sunny went off by herself. She dropped into a crouch as if she were guarding a basketball player. She closed her eyes. Suddenly she called: "Yes!"

Then they all heard: A distant hum of wheel on concrete, followed then by tiny, high-pitched voices:

"Wheeeee!"

"Yahoooo!"

"Fasterrrr!"

Eddie took a deep breath and pierced the night with his silver whistle. Houselights went on along the block; front doors opened. Sunny snatched the whistle from Eddie's neck. "Will you shut up!"

"Okay," whispered Pickles, still listening, "now where?"

They listened some more. Sunny pointed across the street. "Over there somewhere. Definitely."

Pickles was trotting. "Let's go."

Not wanting to go through strange backyards, they ran down to the end of the block, turned left, another block, another left. They halted.

"This is where they were," said Sunny.

"Yeah," huffed Eddie, *were.*"

"*Fasterrrrr!*"

Sunny pointed. "That way!"

Ooguh! Ooguh!

"They found the horn!" Pickles cried. "Come on!"

The chase zipped and dashed in fractured rectangles along the dark streets of Cedar Grove until at last the baby-sitters had the hijackers in sight. They were on the edge of downtown now. There were more lights. They passed Evergreen Bank, Little Flower Shoppe, Hans's Bakery. The hijackers were a block ahead.

Sunny shoved the whistle back at Eddie. "Now!"

Eddie blew. They yelled together, "Stop!"

The hijackers looked back to see their pursuers a half block behind and closing fast. They screamed and leapt from the picklebus, which went on rolling driverless till it coasted off-line and bumped to a stop against the steps of Coletto's Drugstore.

Pickles jumped aboard, and they continued the chase for another half-block, whereupon the hijackers abruptly veered right, bounded up the steps of a building, and burst through the door.

The pursuers paused on the steps. Eddie looked up. "What's that?"

Mounted above the door was the large wooden head of a long-faced, antlered animal.

"That," said Pickles, "is a moose."

"This is where Bobo came," said Salem.

Behind the door music was playing. They went in.

28

"Where's the bingo?" said Sunny.

There was dim lighting, and there was a small band playing slow, old-fashioned music, and there were people dancing in a slow, old-fashioned way, and there were round tables with red tablecloths and huge red hearts swooping from the ceiling on braided red-and-white crepe paper streamers — but there was no bingo.

As they stood inside the doorway, Sunny pointed, "There!"

It was Wayne, leading his brothers through the shadowy figures on the dance floor. Suddenly he called out, "Sally!" and ran up to a dancing couple.

The baby-sitters approached. Even in the shadowy light, the profile of the man proclaimed his identity. "It's Bobo," said Sunny. "Check the gut." The couple had stopped dancing to listen as Wayne chattered up at them. Then they turned to face the baby-sitters, all four of whom stopped in their tracks. Salem gasped: *"Miss Billups!"*

They came closer, not believing their eyes. "Is it you?" said Salem.

"Sal-*leee*," Wayne whined, "come home with us. We don't like them."

"You're Sally?" said Sunny.

Bobo swept Wayne onto his shoulders. He laughed. "Confession time."

The teacher wore a white dress as satiny as the cover on a heart-shaped candy box. Mookie and Bert clung to her hands. She gave an exaggerated shrug of surrender. "You caught me." She smiled. "Let's get away from the traffic." She led everyone to a corner by the buffet table. "Yes," she said, "I'm Sally."

"And you baby-sit for them?"

"Guilty."

"And you came to the dance," said Sunny, "with *him*?"

Miss Billups gave the bus driver a look they had never seen before, a look that, if it were paper, would have matched the hearts hanging from the ceiling. "Guilty as charged."

The four friends just stared, trying to fit this news into the world they thought they knew.

"And you — " said Salem, feeling the shape, the surface of the truth, feeling for the opening to the heart.

"Yes?"

"Was there one Love Line in *The Wurple*, by any chance, that wasn't from a student?"

"Bingo," said Bobo.

The teacher laughed and clapped her hands. "Yes!"

Salem pointed. "SB."

The teacher bowed. "Sarah Billups. Also known as Sally."

Salem turned, gaping, to her teacher's portly dancing partner.

"Students," said Miss Billups, "may I present Mr. Al Krumplik." She laid her head on his shoulder, she fluttered her eyes, she sighed romantically. "My valentine."

The hearts above seemed to swoon, woodwinds wooed.

"Let's go home," said Bobo. He grinned at the baby-sitters. "Unless you want to stay and dance with each other."

Sunny bolted for the door. "For-*get* it!"

In the crowded car, the kids all sat in back, hijackers on baby-sitters' laps.

"You weren't really mad at him at Valley Forge that day, were you?" said Pickles.

Miss Billups turned in the front seat. "No. In fact, he arranged to be the driver for the field trip."

"And he wasn't really sent to Late Room."

"Well," she chuckled, "he was, but not for being late. We happen to have a very nice and understanding and cooperative principal."

"And it wasn't a coincidence that you both just happened to be at the mall that Saturday."

"A well-organized plot."

Salem gasped. "That valentine candy box. You said — "

The teacher smiled and nodded to the driver. "My little nephew."

By the time they pulled up to the house, Miss Billups had told them how she and Bobo — "Al," she called him — had met one day when he honked his school bus at her.

"We never meant to keep it a secret from you kids forever," she said. "But for the time being, we thought it best not to announce to a school full of students that the bus driver and the social studies teacher were going steady."

The baby-sitters agreed that that was definitely a wise decision.

In the backyard, the fire had gone out. Bobo fetched every spare blanket in the house and, well before midnight, seven kids — three little, four big — were asleep in the tent.

Hours later Pickles awoke. He listened to the dark breathings around him. What had awakened him? He stood, keeping the patchwork quilt wrapped about him. He felt his way through the sleepers to the flap in front. He pulled it open. He looked. He put his hand out. He smiled. He whispered, softly as flakefall: "Snow."

29

There were a hundred sleds on Heller's Hill next day, but only one pickleboggan. And everyone wanted to ride it.

Pickles was generous, especially with the little kids. For one plunge down the endless slope, he managed to cram fifteen little bodies, besides himself, between the green panels.

Most of the trips, of course, were reserved for Eddie, Salem, and Sunny — plus a certain bus driver, a social studies teacher, and three former hijackers, all of whom happily showed up on the hill.

When Bobo rode, there was room left for only his girlfriend and the "Captain," which Pickles insisted on being called by anyone aboard the boggan. Whenever Bobo rode, the entire hill stopped to watch. His weight gave to the sled an unstoppable momentum that sent it faster and faster downhill until the silver runners blurred into the sun-dazzled snow.

While others cheered the speed and wonder of the great green rocket, Salem discovered something else — recovery — in the sight of Bobo and Miss Billups flying down the hill together. In their hugging and laughing descent she found the romance that she had so wanted for herself. Miss Billups' happiness, it turned out, was all the valentine she needed.

As for Sunny, her attention was directed elsewhere, namely off to the side, where Tuna Casseroli and his fellow nickelheads were rolling a ball of snow down the hill. By the time it got to the bottom, the ball was as tall as Tuna and twice as fat. A smaller, basketball-size snowball was placed on top. Stones made a doughboy face. A pair of pinecones became earrings. For the hairdo, someone brought a handful of small, round cookies. These were pressed all around the noggin, and presto — snow nickelhead!

Sunny could not resist. She dragged Pickles and his boggan over to the side. She pointed down the hill. "Can you steer this thing real close to that stupid snow jerk?"

"Watch me," he said.

They dragged the sled to the topmost point of the hill and began to push together. Within seconds, they were sprinting. They hopped aboard.

With Pickles manning the tiller, Sunny pulled herself onto the flanks so that one foot rested on the sideboard, one on the backboard. She stood, wobbled, extended her arms for balance, and let out a war cry.

When the nickelheads, who were gathered about their snowman, looked up, they saw a girl straddling Pickles Johnson's green monster like a trick rider in a circus — and it was all hurtling straight down at them. They scattered. As the boggan flew past, they heard the girl yell, "Hai-YAH!" and throw out her leg. The white head exploded in a splatter of cookies and snow.

The action threw Sunny from the sled. When she finally rolled to a stop and looked up, she found herself surrounded by nickelheads. She stood. She pointed at Tuna Casseroli. "That," she snarled, "was for Salem's hat."

What happened next surprised all who witnessed it. The fierce scowl vanished from Tuna's face, and suddenly he was booming with laughter at the sight of his headless snowman and the girl who did it.

Was it the blanketing, peacemaking power of the long-awaited snow? Was it the spell of Valentine's Day? Whatever, within minutes nickelheads were lining up at the top of the hill for rides on the pickleboggan. And every one of them called the driver "Captain."

About the Author

Jerry Spinelli is the author of several novels, including *Fourth Grade Rats*, *The Library Card*, *Do the Funky Pickle*, and the Newbery Medal–winning *Maniac Magee*. He lives in Phoenixville, Pennsylvania, with his wife and fellow author, Eileen Spinelli, and their children.

Any Way You Look At It,

LOUIS SACHAR'S

Books are Hilarious